"The little coyote could not have managed to go much farther. She faltered and staggered several times. Soon she would give up and sink silently on the hot earth to die...."

But that was not to be the fate of Coyote, the Wonder Wolf. Her amazing adventures began when she was rescued from death and shipped from Arizona to the East in a chicken coop. The Horton family received her with great pleasure and fascination and tried to the best of their ability to care for her. But one night, crazed with fear, Coyote broke away and returned to the wild. Her life was a constant struggle for existence, including the job of raising her own family, fighting other wild animals, men, and the violent forces of nature itself.

Coyote,
the Wonder Wolf

Coyote, the Wonder Wolf

by *Joseph Wharton Lippincott*

Illustrated by Ed Dodd

J. B. LIPPINCOTT COMPANY
Philadelphia and New York

Coyote,
the Wonder Wolf

Chapter 1

Evening was dimming the glare of the Arizona land-scape of scrawny bushes and cacti. Soon the sun would move below the horizon on its way around the earth, to appear in the morning over a ridge of low, bare mountains. A red car with black top was moving along the highway leading to the city of Tucson, only a few miles ahead; an ordinary car in looks and action except that it contained, besides two people in the front, a large wire crate that covered more than half of the rear seat. In this crate crouched a brownish-gray animal resembling a small, hairy dog. But this creature looked so thin it seemed to be all skin and bones, and its long, sharp nose appeared out of proportion to its body.

The man and his wife in the front seat glanced back occasionally to see whether the caged animal was all right. At such times the two straw-colored eyes behind the long nose looked back unwinkingly.

"Are you sure you're doing the right thing?" the woman suddenly asked. "A wild coyote for children who've been raised in the East, where these wolves just aren't seen? The children probably don't know they're dangerous. If they treat him like a puppy, he'll likely bite off a finger or a toe or something. Why not let him loose right here in the desert and avoid any trouble?"

"In the first place, Eliza, it isn't a he. It's a she. You heard the Indian. In the second place, she cost me six dollars. And, thirdly, we have to bring those kids some kind of a present, and what would be better coming from the West than a little, young wolf for their menagerie. The kids will be pleased, your sister and brother-in-law will be pleased, the coyote will positively rejoice at having a good home, and your Uncle Harry will be thanked from the bottom of their hearts!"

"I give up," murmured his wife.

"Of course you do," said Uncle Harry.

And that is how a miserable, half-starved little coyote, just a wolf of the plains, happened to be brought to two boys and their parents who lived on a country place at the north edge of Philadelphia. It was an area of farms, woods, and beautiful parks. Rows and rows of city houses threatened to engulf it on two sides and blot out forever most of the natural greenery of that part of William Penn's land.

The young coyote was the last of a litter of six that had been born in a burrow part way up the rocky side of a steep little hill in the desert. There the hard-working wolf mother had nursed the six for weeks, ranged the desert for miles in catching rats, mice, and gophers, rabbits, birds, and lizards, and had even visited some of the garbage heaps that a few scattered houses along the highway afforded. The young ones' coyote father had worked too, but not in such a determined way.

Then it happened—the great calamity. One of the

settlers along the road had brought some chickens from town. These enjoyed ranging a strip of parched ground back of the house until discovered by the coyotes. The first to see them was the father, who at once stalked and easily caught a silly white hen at the edge of the flock. He carried her dead body swiftly to the waiting pups, who were old enough to leave the den and were lying snugly with their mother at the rocky base of the hill, hungrily waiting for safe twilight. They came running and attacked the hen in a ravenous horde, even gulping down feathers and partly chewed bones. Then they looked around for more.

The father started back to the flock of chickens, and with him went the mother, very anxious to satisfy her young. This time each of them caught a hen, while the remaining birds ran loudly squawking, to the house and aroused the owners. On the following day no chickens were visible, but that night the entire coyote family, hopefully hunting the vicinity, came upon many small pieces of fresh meat. These the two older coyotes unhesitatingly began to bolt, one at a time—the young ones fighting each other over some they found among the cactus clumps.

The meat had a strange flavor that the coyotes had never before encountered, but they realized its dangers too late. In minutes, one after another began to roll in agony. The mother, father, and five of the litter did not recover from the powerful poison in the meat chunks.

Only the smallest pup, who had been cruelly elbowed away from the chunks by her eager brothers and sisters, survived. She did not know what had happened to the others, but she had sensed their suffering and was smart enough to associate it with the unusual odor of the meat.

When the sun rose over the ridge, she was crouching close to her mother's lifeless form, which lay stretched out among the creosote bushes. That was where the man in the house saw her when he looked out of the window. It did not take him long to get his gun and step cautiously out of the door.

The little coyote saw him coming, hesitated uncertainly for a few moments waiting for her mother to move, then turned to run alone. The loud bang of the gun and the stinging shot came almost together. The little coyote yelped in surprise and pain, spun around, then ran. Instinctively she headed for the deserted den, the excited man leaping after her and yelling furiously. She increased her speed to its utmost, tumbled over a loose stone, rubbed against bushes, hurt herself on the pin-sharp spines of cacti, but never stopped going. The gun sounded loudly once more, but too far behind to hurt her again, and finally she reached the den and staggered in. That was where she still hid when darkness came.

Far back in the earth she cowered miserably for hours. Never had she felt so thirsty and hungry, so sore in every part of her thin little body. In vain she listened for her parents and sniffed in the directions where her brothers and sisters had always been before this. Toward morning she moved to the den's entrance and looked around. After a time she slunk out and picked up the discarded leg bone of a rabbit. Gnawing this helped quiet her stomach. She slunk out once more and picked up other dried bones scattered around the den. All that day she crouched in the farthest, darkest corner, listening intently but hearing nothing. Thirst and hunger continued to plague her. Night brought nothing new.

In the early morning she walked in desperation a short distance from the den. Here she flopped down and rested, her chin between her front paws. Out came the bright sun and began to heat up the parched ground and everything on it. Soon she was forced to move and find shade, but where should she go? On and on she walked, scarcely knowing that she was moving. An old coyote would have found shade somewhere, perhaps behind a rock or a cactus or under a particularly large desert bush or in a hole. He would have scratched the earth a little and made a comfortable, cool bed. Even the rattlesnake had to escape the blazing sun.

The little coyote could not have managed to go much farther. She faltered and staggered several times. She whimpered forlornly every few minutes, and once yapped dismally with her nose in the air. Soon she would give up and sink silently on the hot earth to die.

Perhaps Nature, which governs so many things, had, however, not intended that she should die this way, but it did not shield her from the sun or lead her to water and food. Instead, by chance, the little coyote staggered in front of an Indian, a very old man, slowly making his way across the desert to his shack beside the highway. A white man might have killed the little creature, but not an Indian, for he and his forefathers had had no angry feeling toward the wolves.

The coyote could not run away. She tried, then sank down on the ground and hid her head, eyes closed, behind the stem of a bush. Her heart almost stopped beating as she waited.

The old Indian stood over her, wondering what he should do. He saw that she was completely worn out and starving and he knew that she would need many meals before she could fend for herself in the desert. He did not have food to spare. So he looked around him helplessly, then up into the sky as if searching for an answer to his problem.

Now Nature may have decreed that at this very moment a golden eagle appear high in the air, soaring in circles, watching everything below. The old Indian shaded his eyes, the better to see the big bird. He knew that if he deserted the little coyote the eagle would soar lower, then suddenly descend like a rocket with claws spread. The old man could not bear the idea of seeing the

helpless pup borne away shrieking. Quickly, then, he knelt down, placed gnarled thumb and index finger around the coyote's neck, and lifted the animal cautiously. Pressing her bony body gently against his hip, he carried her toward his home.

Chapter 2

WATER! That was what the coyote needed most, and what the Indian laid before her. On it floated small pieces of bread that had been dipped in melted grease. This she sniffed timidly, then took down the bread in gulps as soon as the Indian moved away. She had never seen a brook or a lake or water in any usual form and had never lapped up liquids. Always moisture had come in her mother's milk or later in regurgitated food laid before her, and in the freshly killed animals and birds she had eaten. Bread she had not seen and might not have eaten by itself, but the grease on it reassured her. Its smell in the water seemed wonderful!

Soon she was walking guardedly around the Indian's one-room dwelling, exploring, examining new objects, using her nose to verify what her eyes told her. The door was closed. There was only one window, and that, too, was closed. She stayed away from the Indian, but felt no special fear of him unless he made a quick movement or came toward her. Her parents had never warned her against man, and she had not seen very clearly the one who had shot at her.

Presently she lay down in a corner behind a large chair, her eyes, however, always watching the Indian. To let her get acquainted with water, he placed some without bread on the floor in a saucer and some also in a bowl. He was sure that soon she would notice it, find it good, and learn to lap. Later he took a bucket from the bench back of his house and walked to the small store a short distance down the road to get more water. Here he told about the coyote pup and received a handout of kitchen scraps.

On the following morning, the Indian arose at dawn from his crude cot and began the day by tossing scraps to the coyote. And very soon the little wolf was eating ravenously. Reassured, the man opened the door wide and gave the coyote a perfect chance to escape, but she would not leave her corner behind the chair. This somehow pleased the Indian. After that, the door remained open.

Several days passed. They were much like the first except that the pup had moved out of the house and made a bed under a large bush fifty steps away. The Indian continued to feed her scraps and to put out water in the bowl. Then one day while he was throwing the scraps a red car with a black top drew up beside the house and the driver, Uncle Harry, called, "Is anyone there? Hello there! Hello!"

The Indian was not sure whether to answer. But Uncle Harry had glimpsed him and now stepped out of the car and walked around to the rear of the house, where the Indian had just tossed a crust to the coyote, who was waiting among the creosote bushes.

"Hi!" called Uncle Harry. Then he saw the little

coyote. "Well, I declare!" he exclaimed. "A coyote youngster!" But at once the pup hid behind her favorite bush and watched this stranger through the lower branches.

"My car needs water in the radiator, just enough to take us to the nearest garage. Will you help us?"

The Indian nodded and picked up the water bucket.

"I say," Uncle Harry exclaimed, thinking hard, "is that a tame coyote? Is it for sale?"

The Indian hesitated, then answered, "I can catch coyote if you want it."

Uncle Harry, being a man of action, quickly decided that he did want it, so the Indian shuffled down the road to the man whose chickens had been raided by the coyotes, and secured the wire coop in which they had been brought from town.

It took a lot of coaxing with scraps to get the always-hungry pup inside the house, but that night the old Indian did it, and next day Uncle Harry got his coyote, all safe in the chicken coop. Everybody was happy except Uncle Harry's wife and the little wolf.

Some days later, Uncle Harry arrived in the East and was able to present the coyote pup to the Horton family. They were a very unusual family, indeed. Their house seemed swarming with dogs and cats, and outside were geese, ducks, chickens, and a number of small pens or cages containing rabbits and guinea pigs, woodchucks and squirrels. Noise seemed to worry no one. Barks, meows, squeals, quacks and cackling blended together in a great hodgepodge of sound.

Into this atmosphere the frightened little coyote was lugged in her wire coop and was escorted by Mr. and

Mrs. Horton and their two sons to a small enclosed shed at the rear of the house. This had once been a pigeon coop. It consisted of two stories; one side was wire mesh from ground to roof. In the rear was a barrel, placed on its side and facing the wall, to serve as a retreat and a bed. And behind this barrel ran the coyote as soon as her coop was opened.

"What a fine little fellow!" boomed Mr. Horton.

"It's a she," announced Uncle Harry.

"Of course, of course," agreed Mr. Horton. "What do you name a she-coyote?"

The two boys looked at him. "We've already decided on just 'Coyote,'" one of them said.

"O.K.," Mr. Horton replied. "Just fine. Now you have a little wild wolf named Coyote. Not hard to remember either. But don't forget to feed him—I mean her. And don't give him—I mean her—a chance to bite. She's a wolf, remember!" Laughingly he turned to Uncle Harry. "Thanks to you our zoo business is beginning to boom. It's going to be good for the boys and their friends to learn something about wolves before there are none left on the plains."

The little coyote received a bucket of water in her pen, some corn bread, and a dead mouse from a trap. She did not leave her barrel until night, then she spent her time trying in every way possible to get out of the enclosure. She scratched and chewed, climbed and jumped, but all in vain.

After their breakfast the boys opened her door and came into the pen. They had scraps of ham to throw to her, and they routed her out of her barrel to see if she was all right. In wild fear she rushed around the enclosure, then quieted down and crouched in a corner. The boys soon left to work at the nearby pens.

After more than a week the coyote became really tame. She plucked food from the boys' hands and never retreated to her barrel when they appeared. She learned to climb up the wire and to use the second floor, the shelf where the pigeons once had nested. She had already grown stouter and sleeker, but every night when all was quiet she tried to get out of the pen.

The Hortons owned three small fox terriors. These never missed an opportunity to run along the wire of the coyote's pen, barking shrilly if she was in sight. The four cats took no interest in her, but she watched them whenever they came out of the house. In fact, she watched everything that moved, even the sparrows and the larger insects, particularly the butterflies. She was learning, educating herself.

She became so tame that the boys were able to teach her to wear a collar and to be led. After that, they took her on walks around the countryside, making sure, however, that no dogs came near. The terriers had to be tied up at home. Everywhere she went she sniffed at almost everything. If a cottontail jumped from its hiding place, she tried to chase it. When once she spied a running woodchuck she leaped after it so suddenly that she pulled the lead strap out of the hand of one of the boys. The chuck was in a pasture twenty yards away, but before he could reach his burrow on the far side of the fence, she was beside him.

Not knowing just where to seize him, she nipped at his rump. That stopped him but gave him a chance to turn and bury his four front teeth in her leg. She did not yelp.

She shook him off and danced around him now. Again and again she nipped and sprang away while testing the length of his thrust. He was about half grown, well furred, and weighed nearly five pounds, and he had been in fights before. Always he kept his mind on reaching his burrow, so he sidled toward it at every opportunity and suddenly was near enough to bolt in.

The coyote did not know about the burrow and was greatly surprised to see him vanish and escape. She sniffed at the deep hole slanting into the ground, and listened intently when he chattered at her tauntingly from a safe distance below. Then she began to dig, and such was her desire to get the chuck that she could scarcely be pulled away.

Every day after that she tugged at the lead until she reached the pasture and could look around for the chuck. Twice more she saw him and was allowed to rush after him, but too late to keep him from his burrow. Then the boys got an idea. They kept the lead strap fastened to her collar but let her run with it dragging loose. This allowed her to hunt more freely in the grass and the bushes. On the third day she found and caught the chuck after a furious run. This time she got him by the neck, the hold safely away from those long rodent teeth, and she did not let go.

Breathing fast, she rested beside his body, then dragged him as far as a fence corner and carefully buried him. Instinctively she knew that in that way she could save his meat until she was hungry.

When the boys told Mr. Horton about this, he was worried.

"She's not yet full grown and really strong," he said,

"but she's beginning to learn that she's a wolf. If one of our dogs tangles with her, I'm sorry for him. She's not going to be bullied any more. And I don't think you can stop her when she's started something. Hadn't you better just leave her in the pen?"

But the boys were very fond of Coyote. There was always something lovable about her, and her evident trust and willingness to follow them appealed to their vanity. They took her out for a ramble every afternoon, giving her the opportunity to gain knowledge she was not to forget about the surrounding fields and woods. But when they called she would come to them, prancing about and wagging her tail in great good humor. She was like a pet dog but more interesting.

Rats and mice abounded around the pens and when caught in traps added to Coyote's ration of dog chow. She liked the mice especially, and spent much time in trying to catch them for herself when any sought crumbs in her quarters. She learned to hide herself and lie in wait for some of the little things, and to stalk others. She could scoop them up easily from the floor of the pen because her two long teeth in the front of her lower jaw were farther forward than those in the upper jaw. The clever rats were too wary to give her any good chances.

Now during the day she spent much of her time crouching on the narrow top floor of the pigeon pen. Here she could watch all that was going on around her and see everyone as they approached. When visitors came, she flattened herself against the boards and tried not to be noticed. Strangers always alarmed her and no offerings of food from them could tempt her to come down. This high perch became her favorite hiding place.

When chilly autumn nights arrived, Coyote's thick winter coat of fur began to grow fast. In November it was beautiful. The general color was gray-brown, but there were black hairs on the shoulders and white hairs on the breast. Enough stiff long hairs grew through the soft fur to keep it in place and protect it. It shed rain perfectly. Now she looked filled out, almost stout. When curled up in a ball, with her long, fluffy tail wrapped around her nose and feet, she could sleep without feeling winter's cold. Unlike her, the terriers, whose hair was short, had to be given warm quarters.

When snows came, Coyote developed a new trick. She caught sparrows and starlings. Many of these birds, unable to forage satisfactorily in the fields and streets, drifted about, seeking grain wherever they could find it. In the Horton pens were plenty of scraps that lured these small birds through the wide-mesh wire barriers. The coyote delighted in feigning sleep and dashing at the birds when they grew too bold. She would leap into the air to seize them as they tried to fly away. They were eaten feathers and all.

But other creatures were affected by the snow and cold. Dogs that had grown half wild and had delighted in ranging the countryside together, killing rabbits, pheasants, and other game during much of the year, now found less to amuse them. The rabbits were holed up and other creatures scarce. One night when the moon was shining, four of these, all large dogs with hound or police-dog blood in their veins to give them the roving and hunting instinct, raided the Horton pens. They scented what was inside and tore through the fencing around the rabbits and guinea pigs, killing what they could, then they gathered in an excited, almost crazed pack around the coyote pen. Here they dug and pulled at the wire barrier determined to reach and finish the coyote, too.

So far, in spite of all that had been going on, there had not been enough noise to awaken the Horton family, and if one of the dogs, a brown, hairy half-breed, had not managed to get into the henhouse and upset barrels and pans in chasing the squawking chickens, the coyote might have been killed. But in the henhouse the racket was tremendous. The dogs with one exception left the coyote pen to join in the chasing and killing of fluttering, running, and flying fowl. Some chickens were managing to get out of the house and run blindly over the snow with barking dogs in close pursuit. Two flew into trees.

The police dog that stayed at the coyote pen was so intent on his work of digging that he took no interest in the uproar. The ground under the snow was only partly frozen and so full of gravel and small stones that he could make real headway. All at once he found that he could thrust his head under the wire, then his shoulders and long, strong body. At last he was inside the pen, sniffing and looking.

The coyote was hiding on her shelf overhead, but there he quickly found her by scent. Rising on hind legs, he looked over the edge of the shelf and right into the eyes of his quarry! There was one moment of indecision, then a wild bark and a leap to get up to her. This was fun for him; just a little coyote at bay, something to chase and maul in the manner of his wolf ancestors.

She jumped over the dog's head to the ground. He snapped at her body, missed, and nearly turned over backward. Then around the pen they raced. How she could dodge and twist and leap! Again and again he cornered her, only to have her escape his teeth. But he sensed that if he kept this up he could catch her. She had nowhere to hide, nowhere to go.

The uproar among the chickens was stopped suddenly. While others of the family watched from windows, Mr. Horton descended on the scene with a flashlight and a walking stick. He could swing the stick with great accuracy and he was mad enough to want to hurt any and all dogs. One of them he hit across the rear. Another he smote full on the chest. Both rolled over but regained their feet and ran away, with him chasing them as fast as he could go.

But since he was losing ground, Mr. Horton turned to the other pens and saw the big dog in the coyote's enclosure. He ran toward it but could not get into the pen without giving the dog and the coyote a chance to escape. However, he frightened the dog and made it forget the coyote. Now it had a vengeful man to deal with and at once it bared its teeth. With his hand on the latch of the pen's gate, Mr. Horton looked at the dog and the dog looked back at him, growling low and dangerously. The dog was at bay. It would fight.

The man thought hard. He was no coward, but he saw the dog's point of view. Since it was cornered, it was desperate. He opened the gate and stepped aside. Out dashed the dog and over the snow it ran. The man turned toward the chicken house, looked again at the sad, desolate sight and forgot all about Coyote's gate.

Chapter 3

I N THE morning the boys sadly announced to their
father that, in addition to the havoc among the chickens and small pets, they found that Coyote was gone.

After breakfast he took his account book from its shelf
and wrote in it:

> Loss— 8 chickens
>   6 rabbits
>   15 guinea pigs
>   1 coyote

"It was lucky that we had eaten the geese and ducks,"
he mused.

When the boys came home from school, they met
their father returning from his office.

"News, Dad," called Tom, the elder of the two.
"Jimmy Murphy says their fine dog isn't feeling too
good today. And, oh yes! Tommy Flint told us his father
thought their dog had been sideswiped by a truck!"
Then Tom asked, "Dad, did you get the dog that was
after Coyote?"

His father was looking at him very seriously indeed.

But when he answered, a twinkle came into his eyes.

"Boys," he boomed, "the big dog that tried to kill Coyote got clear away. And" he added, "I'm afraid he won't change his evil ways, and I have a feeling—just a queer feeling—that sometime in his carefree rambling he'll make a mistake and maybe give Coyote a chance to get even."

"Then you think Coyote is all right and will keep on living somewhere in the woods?"

"I certainly do," answered his father. "I think you'll hear a lot from that coyote." How very right he later proved to be.

Not only had the gate of the coyote's pen been left open, but also there was the dog's hole under the wire. Had the coyote not been so frightened and nervous, she might not have wanted to leave her home pen. But now her one thought was to get to open country where she could not again be cornered. True, she hesitated at the gate, but not for long. When she stepped out, she began at once to run, and this she kept up until the open fields were passed and she was in the half-gloom of the nearest wood. There she slowed down to a cautious walk.

The air that night was not very cold, and when she crouched down, the better to look and listen, her fur made her feel quite warm. She heard the far-off night sounds of civilization, the endless purr of automobiles, a dog's distant bark, the harsh toot of an electric train. Everything was reassuring. Her nerves were calm now.

She knew this wood from recent rambles, and remembered that at the far side the big trees gave way to bushes and great masses of honeysuckle vines that could make a good hiding place for any wild animal even in winter, for most of the leaves remained on the vines. Rabbits and deer ate these leaves, meadow mice nibbled the bark of the vines close to the ground, where the little creatures were well hidden from owls. Here and there a deserted bird's nest showed that in summer, too, the vines were useful.

Coyote pushed into the biggest group of clumps she could find, and scratched away the snow to make a better bed. Before she lay down she made sure that if necessary she could run in almost any direction. Satisfied now, she rolled into a ball and slept.

The coyote did not realize what a serious step she was taking in cutting herself off from regular handouts of food and excellent protection. Love of freedom had coursed in her veins, and now that she had run away, it was for always. She would never willingly leave freedom behind and return to live in a cramped enclosure. The police dog had done that to her, changed her world, altered her future life. In a few hours she had irrevocably become again part and parcel of the wild.

Coyote was hungry. It was early morning and day was breaking. She had been awake for some time but felt so strange in her new surroundings that she lay low. A few birds were stirring in the trees and bushes; to her they were new birds, not like the sparrows and the starlings. Fascinated, she watched a red cardinal scurry about, and a downy woodpecker hammer loudly on a dead limb. A gray squirrel came slowly, head first down a nearby oak, cautiously but with a confident air. He hunted in the snow for acorns he had buried, smelled one, dug down through the snow and leaves, clawed it out of the earth, and dashed up the oak with it, held by his front teeth. There Coyote heard him shelling it, dropping pieces of husk until he could gnaw the kernel.

Everything was a first now. The first cardinal, the first woodpecker, the first gray squirrel, the first red-tailed hawk sailing over the trees, the first chickadee in the birches, and so it went. Two small winter animals the coyote knew something about—mice and rabbits. When she walked out of the honeysuckle she scented mice, but could not see any. Tracing the odor through the snow, she came over a spot where a meadow mouse, or vole, a little grass and bark eater, was burrowing along the ground under the snow. Instinctively she leaped on it with her front feet and forced her nose through the snow until she could seize the mouse held down by her paws. Swallowed whole, it made a good start for breakfast.

For the next hour, she hunted meadow mice along the edge of the woodland and caught two more before they stopped moving around in their own feeding. They were full grown, four inches long and, as usual, very fat and juicy. Water she secured by chewing snow.

When the warmth of the sun made the woods pleasant, two dogs came through on a hunting expedition of their own. One was a brown and black Airedale, the other a tan and white beagle. They used teamwork. When the beagle poked about the bushes with his very keen nose, the Airedale circled to catch any rabbit that was flushed.

The coyote, hearing them approach, crouched in the honeysuckle. But the beagle caught her scent and went in to investigate. This scent was something entirely new to him and interesting. The odor was strong. He glanced around to make sure that the Airedale was near to back him up, then he forced his way into the honeysuckle clumps. The coyote rose to her feet to meet him. Here she saw just a small dog no larger than herself and perhaps friendly.

When the beagle came suddenly upon her he was greatly surprised. She looked like a dog, but she did not smell like one. He stood uncertainly, looking at her. She wagged her tail and sidled around in front of him. Still he was undecided about her. Then up came the large Airedale, to regard the coyote with utmost curiosity and suspicion. He was not a bit timid and therefore advanced stiffly. Coyote moved away just enough to keep at a safe distance.

The Airedale felt contemptuous and showed this in the usual dog manner, then scratched the snow with his hind feet. Had the coyote run away, both dogs would have chased her, but she just sidled about or stood looking at them. Gradually the dogs lost interest. They did not quite understand what this new kind of creature was doing in their hunting country, but they saw no fun in pushing a fight.

When the dogs resumed their rabbit hunting, Coyote followed them at a distance. She saw them flush a rabbit; she watched the beagle trail the cottontail and the Airedale try to head it off. The rabbit escaped into an old woodchuck burrow and the two dogs, after a little useless digging, wandered on. But beside the burrow crouched the coyote in wait for the rabbit to come out. She had patience, and in the first gloom of evening, saw the rabbit cautiously sneak out. In one dash she caught him. Her first major kill for food, an important conquest.

Every few days in December she saw the Airedale and

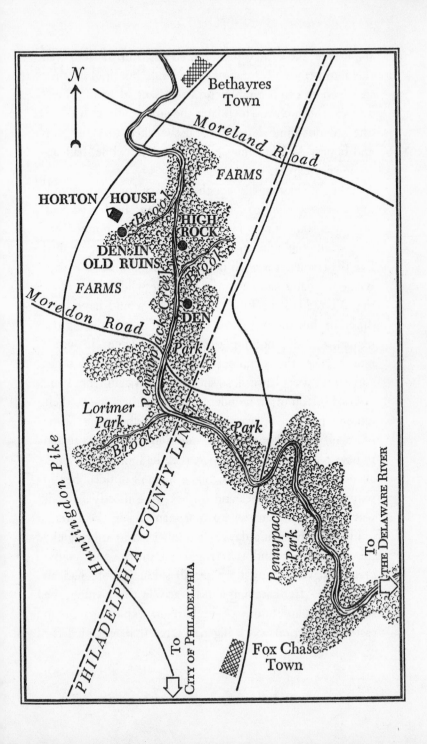

the beagle. Now they just ignored her. But she followed them and took advantage of their able hunting! If they managed to catch a rabbit or a pheasant, they often left parts of the carcass which later the coyote ate with relish. She did not mind leftovers and she liked to chew skin and bones. And her mouse hunting, meanwhile, had become very expert.

At night she ranged over the country for miles, avoiding houses as well as all humans. Why she feared man now was something of a mystery. No one noticed her during all that winter, no one knew that what seemed like the tracks of a small dog, in woods and fields everywhere, actually had been made by one wild coyote from the West. Had she killed chickens, it would have been different, but she was cautious, moved mostly during the nights, and did nothing to arouse suspicion. It was a mouse year; their numbers were at a peak, and other game, too, was plentiful, so she needed no help from man. Mr. Horton often wondered what had become of their onetime pet, but he was not very happy about the escape of a wolf and did not raise the question. The boys seemed to have forgotten all about her; they had many new pets, all now in dogproof pens. Since no one noticed her in winter, when the trees and bushes were mostly bare, it was no wonder that she was not seen during the spring.

In the early spring days when hibernating animals like the woodchuck and the frog came forth, and young creatures were being born on all sides, Coyote had an easy time. After catching a meal early in the evening, she spent more and more of each night exploring. In an easterly direction was a big park area that extended for miles on each side of a creek, the Pennypack, a favorite place for picnickers and Boy Scouts.

At night this was deserted by man, but not by the wild creatures, who were legally protected within its limits. White-tailed deer hid by day in its thickets; foxes, raccoons, and opossums, skunks, muskrats, and weasels traveled along the water's edge at night. Several kinds of frogs and turtles, fishes and snakes could be seen in or around the stream. And birds abounded. There were high rocks, steep banks, and bush-covered sections everywhere. Soon the coyote knew almost every foot of Lorimer Park and the connecting Pennypack Park. And soon she became acquainted with the wild animals that regularly lived there.

Chapter 4

Coyote saw the same animals again and again, for they did not go far from their home territory. She often met two gray foxes that hunted together, and she came regularly upon an old buck and four does. She knew the den trees of the gray squirrels and the favorite thickets of each rabbit. Along the creek she saw the same raccoons, skunks, and opossums. And they in turn recognized her. There was an armed truce between her and the other meat eaters, and also between her and the deer. These could put up a fight against a single coyote and they knew it.

In the case of the rabbits, muskrats, and all small grass and nut eaters it was different. These hid or ran away at her approach.

Coyote feared only humans and their large dogs. Also she was at first in awe of cats, regardless of their color. Their stealthy way of hunting in the woods sometimes brought her suddenly face to face with one. At other times she would almost step on a cat that was crouched in the long grass watching for a mouse, a bird, or a small rabbit. Once she came upon a huge gray cat that had caught a young robin and was about to eat it as the parent birds screamed overhead. The surprised cat instantly leaped at her and scratched her nose with both front paws. At the same time it made a furious spitting sound and puffed out its fur to make it look as big and formidable as possible.

Leaping to one side, Coyote stood studying this angry creature, which now crouched and let forth a steady, whining growl. Then it was Coyote who angrily sprang, nipping and leaping away. Instantly the big cat lost its nerve and ran in great leaps, leaving the robin to the coyote.

Next she made friends with a red fox who was without a mate. He and the gray foxes disliked each other, but he and the coyote met so often in their lonely hunting that they began to hunt together and use teamwork in catching rabbits.

Only twice again did the police dogs appear, and on both occasions they found Coyote and chased her. She had to run for her life until out of sight; after that she dodged them in the bushes, then ran fast to a wide but shallow crossing in the creek. The deer, when chased, did the same. Once Coyote saw two run in the middle of the creek for a distance and thus completely confuse their pursuers.

When June brought really hot weather, the heavy, beautiful fur of the coyote and that of the red fox were forced off their bodies by the growth of short summer hair and a small amount of short fur. The two looked mangy for a time, then neat and trim. Now woodticks had a better chance to bury their heads in the skin and suck blood, but fleas became very scarce. Coyote did not often suffer from the various kinds of worms that plague dogs. The great amount of hair and feathers she swallowed helped sweep the intestines clean.

The buck had, as usual, shed his two antlers in January; now Coyote found one and, like the rodents, took a try at gnawing it. She had watched the young new antlers begin to show on his head in April, and would see them become large in July, though swollen-looking and soft and covered with velvet. Later, when September came, she would watch him rub off the drying velvet by butting saplings. At last they would look pointed and formidable again.

The does, sleek and red in their summer coats, had spotted fawns following them in June. One doe had three. When Coyote came near, the does at first would prepare to defend themselves and their young with their front hoofs, but they were ready to run if challenged. Coyote, however, had not learned to molest the big, handsome creatures, though she always watched them.

She met several skunks in her rambles. She disliked their smell and only once came very near one. Noticing a scuffle in the woods, she trotted closer to investigate and found a huge owl trying to kill a black and white skunk. It had fastened its clawed feet on the animal's shoulders and partly paralyzed it but not enough to prevent the discharge of a horrible spray of skunk odor.

The owl was keeping its balance by flapping its wings, and it was dragging the struggling skunk to a more open place. Suddenly it let go and rose in the air to come down on its prey for a better grip, disabling it even further.

Then it saw Coyote and, after glaring at her with its round yellow eyes, flew into a nearby tree. Coyote had never before seen a great horned owl, though she had heard its hoots in the night.

She walked around the skunk, keeping a careful watch on the big owl and trying to avoid the worst of the odor. Then suddenly the owl silently dropped from its perch and flew at her with snapping beak and weird cries. The menacing bird was actually fanning her with its wings.

She ran into the woods, but the skunk odor clung to her legs and she had to roll in the leaves and rub it off on the grass as best she could. Before she lost most of it her interest in skunks was badly shaken.

Coyote stalked crows where they walked in the fields far from cover. These black birds would fly at her with loud cawing whenever they glimpsed her. They were troublemakers and they looked eatable. In the winter she had seen them in wary flocks, but now in July, when the young ones were out of the nest and hungrily following and annoying their parents in their anxiety to be fed, she found them scattered and less wary.

An old crow seemed always on guard and ready to shout an alarm, but when at noon crows came to a brook to drink and bathe, Coyote found better cover. Crawling almost on her stomach and stopping whenever the crows looked around, she drew nearer and nearer. A young one was standing in the shallow stream flapping lustily and making the water fly. Coyote was within a few feet of it before one of the parents saw her, but then it was too late. The young crow tried hard to escape but, being wet, could not rise fast enough. Coyote sprang at it in the air and pulled it down.

At once the other crows made a great fuss. Furiously the old ones dove at the wolf, cawing their loudest but unable to make her let go. Other crows came from all directions and joined the fray. Then Coyote began to run, but only because the noise called attention to her and might have brought men. Now she knew how to catch crows.

The crows, she learned, appointed themselves sentinels of the countryside. Very little escaped their notice, and their loud alarm caw was heeded by all wild animals and birds. Another good alarmist was the blue jay, and still another the killdeer plover of the marsh and meadow. A man out walking, away from roads, was spotted and announced almost immediately. After that, his progress was constantly watched. Animals and birds could easily keep out of his way unless he hid and kept so still for a time that the alarmists' fears were allayed.

Coyote heeded all signals. A squirrel running fast up a tree meant danger unless he was being chased by another squirrel. If he barked at some creature in a suspicious way, it was especially alarming until it could be discovered that he was barking at a fox or cat or raccoon and not at a man. Many kinds of birds cried out when suddenly alarmed. The great blue herons that waded in the creek were so tall and shy that they made excellent spies, as did the wary, loudmouthed mallard ducks.

When the frog army was singing in the early spring, a sudden stillness meant trouble afoot. Running deer, unless playing together, and, in fact, any creatures that ran to gain cover, were all signaling danger. Even insects played a part, in particular those that chirped unless frightened. Coyote lost more than one muskrat because in her stalking she happened on big frogs that leaped into the creek with loud splashes.

No wonder the foxes and the coyote learned to slip through grass and bushes without a sound and without being seen. Dry leaves on the ground often spoiled stalks, but moist leaves, after rains, made stalking much easier and also held the scent of woods creatures.

Once Coyote came upon the Horton family's three terriers. They were alone, snooping along the edge of a wood. She was pleased and immediately anxious to join them. They and she were acquainted and she had forgotten their hostility. Trotting up beside them, she sidled in the friendliest manner, wagging her tail and even whining.

The terriers stood looking at her as if not believing their eyes. Then, all together, they charged with shrill, furious barking. She had to run. Crestfallen, she crouched behind bushes and watched the cocky terriers scratch with hind feet and gloat over their victory. This affair hurt her bitterly. How she longed for friends during all these months in the woods!

The time of plenty was now drawing to a close. Hot weather had come and slowly gone. Now, in September, the nights were cool, rain fell often, and winter was on its way. Coyote was growing her winter fur; so were squirrels and other animals. The red summer coat of the deer was giving way to brownish gray, and the fawns were losing their white spots. The winter sleepers, such as the skunk and the woodchuck, were so fat that they could scarcely run. Young of the year were almost full grown, and both young and old were becoming wild and shy, as if knowing that soon the leaves would fall from all the trees and bushes except evergreens and leave few of the usual hiding places.

While the winter sleepers were growing fat, the gray squirrels, which stayed active all winter, were feverishly gathering and storing nuts, burying them in the ground. The muskrats were adding mud to their winter houses in the marshes, birds were migrating south by day and night, and everywhere was the restless spirit of a changing season.

Chapter 5

ONE MORNING in late October, Coyote heard gunshots before she had retired to her favorite spot
on a high bluff overlooking the Pennypack Creek. She
saw the crows become alarmed and fly high over the
trees, and in the distance she saw flocks of mallards go
speeding down the creek, headed toward the safer waters
of the Delaware River. Soon she heard hounds baying,
more shots and shouting. It was time for her to find a
better hiding place, and she started to run for the dense
thickets in the park area.

She had traveled only a few yards when she caught
sight of two men, in brown clothes and red hats, moving
ominously through the bushes ahead of her. She changed
her direction and, though running more guardedly,
nearly collided with a large brown and white dog. The
dog heard her, looked up inquisitively, and quickly
turned to head her off. Then a black and tan dog appeared, and he too wanted a closer look.

Coyote dodged behind a bush and ran as fast as she
could. She fairly flew over the ground as behind her
came sounds of excited baying and shouting.

"What was it?" called a gruff voice.

"A big fox!" came a reply. "Queer color. Maybe he'll circle."

She was skirting an open field but keeping close to a hedgerow. She sighted two more brown-coated men ahead of her just in time to dodge into the hedgerow. Here she stopped to look around. To be safe, she crawled through the hedge, intending to run along the other side of it. Just then the two dogs came into the field following her trail. They were baying loudly and running fast.

There was no time to lose. Coyote rushed for the woods ahead. Now she nearly lost her life. Another man appeared at the edge of the woods close to her path. She was going so fast that he was taken by surprise and could not aim his gun until she was past and dashing among the bushes. Then he fired.

As in Arizona, she again felt the sudden sting of shot. But it was small shot intended for rabbits and squirrels, so it did not maim her. She flinched but continued her wild pace. In a minute she was in the park, but the hounds were still fast on her trail.

Coyote tried the water trick; she crossed the creek. Ahead of her she saw two deer vanishing in the woods with their white tails straight up. She turned downstream and ran along the far bank, keeping an eye on her back trail. The two hounds came to the water, stopped, sniffed, then floundered across. Coyote was more frightened now and ran for a distant thicket. There she stopped to listen. She could still hear the bugle notes of the hounds. She waited, ready to run again.

The baying continued but came no nearer; in fact it seemed to be going away from her. Eventually she came to understand that the younger hounds were interested only in chasing something and would drop one trail to follow a stronger scent. This time they had taken to the trail of the two deer, who were safe because the hounds were quickly called out of the park.

Not one of the three hunters who had glimpsed Coyote guessed that he had viewed a real wolf. All said that it was an especially big fox, unlike any they had ever seen. How they wished they could have bagged it!

Coyote soon realized that for some reason gunners did not come into the park and that they kept their dogs away from it as much as possible. Day after day the gunning continued. Coyote stayed in the park thickets until nighttime, when it was safe to go into the farm lands and hunt for the many wounded or dead rabbits and pheasants the gunners had not found.

Everything quieted down after a month. The open season for small game had come to an end. Then came a week of deer hunting. The big buck who was cagey enough to stay safely in the middle of the park was the one legal deer that remained in that area. One hunter shot a doe, by mistake, he claimed, and other hunters wounded a fawn that later died in the woods and afforded many a meal to Coyote and the foxes. After that the shooting season ended.

But another danger came with the trapping season. Boys set small traps along the edge of the creek for muskrats and larger ones in the woods for foxes, raccoons, and opossums. Some also set traps in the creek and in smaller streams for raccoons that hunted crayfish and frogs. Traps in the woods were readily detected by Coyote until snow fell and blanked out the odors of metal and of man. She stepped into two that were set in paths, but managed to pull out her feet without being injured. She detected at once those that were baited.

The roving dogs bungled into traps. The police dogs were strong enough to pull free without much trouble, but the Airedale and his beagle companion got caught and had a bad time. Coyote found the Airedale when his left front foot was in a fox trap. He was sensible enough not to struggle madly but to dig and chew at what held him. He pulled the trap's chain free of the stake to which it was fastened and managed to drag it all the way to his home. There, of course, he was relieved of it and was well doctored. The beagle, however, had to wait in a trap until the trapper came on the following morning.

Mr. Horton listened one evening to his sportsmen friends reviewing their shooting of the autumn. Presently the subject came up of the big, brownish-gray fox they had seen. Of course he recognized Coyote from the description and knew then that she was still alive.

"The big fox is certainly a menace to game, I tell you," was one man's verdict. "I've seen its tracks all through the spring and summer. It lives right here in our woods."

Mr. Horton remained very silent. He was exceedingly interested in what he had learned.

Snow did not fall in any large quantity until early in January. Then there was a blizzard. The snow drifted over roads and into gullies until in some places it was ten feet deep. Coyote had trouble in making her way through the woods and in catching rabbits because, while her feet sank deeply, those lighter animals with much fur around their toes could skip over the surface of the

snow. She was hungry and very lonely, lonelier than she had ever felt. Even the foxes were gone, chased away or trapped; she had not seen the red one or the grays for weeks.

Through all these months she had been very silent, content to go her own way and quietly take life as it came to her, but now she felt the urge to look for companionship, and to be on the move. Gone suddenly was any contentment.

Walking out on her favorite high rock overlooking the now frozen creek, she stood for a while looking at the snow scene in the moonlight. A wave of unhappiness came over her. Raising her nose in the air, she howled the great, sad, long-drawn-out howl of loneliness. Again and again the howl resounded over the valley. It seemed to come from nowhere in particular, but it filled the air. Dogs in the neighborhood had never heard anything like it, but they somehow understood and suddenly began to howl in sympathy. In every direction there were yowls, yelps, and barks, some of them from within doors where man's pets retired from the cold.

As suddenly as Coyote had begun, she stopped. She had lost the urge, at least temporarily.

"What happened to start the dogs barking like that?" was the question on all sides.

That night Coyote caught a muskrat. He lived in a hole deep in the bank of the creek, and undertook to burrow under the snow like his relative, the meadow vole, to reach a nearby grassy spot where he could dig up edible roots. Thinking himself safely hidden, he did not hear the coyote approach. One jump in the right spot and Coyote had him. He was twenty-four inches long and he tried to put up a fight, but he was no match for a wolf. Even his bare, scaly tail and his bony feet were chewed and swallowed with his furry hide.

Coyote spent the day in a thicket on the hill among festoons of snow. She was hiding from the crows, who liked to caw at her; also, this was a place from which she could see in almost every direction, sniff all the scents on the breezes. Night found her once more on her favorite high rock, for again loneliness overcame her and she felt the urge to howl and look all around. This time her howling had a slightly different tone; some of the sadness was gone and there was almost a commanding note in her song. Again the dogs howled and barked, and their unobservant owners wondered why.

When the snow was older and its surface had been hardened by the cold, the coyote took a night trip into the farm country. She was sniffing as if more curious than usual or else searching for a special scent. When at length she found this scent she stopped on the lawn of a big house and sat down with a definite purpose—she wanted to howl. And howl she did. After several long howls, lights appeared in some of the windows, then the front door was thrown open and a man's voice shouted, "Go for him, Caesar! Sic 'em, boy!"

A reluctant Airedale was pushed through the doorway. He stood on the mat, unwilling to move farther.

"Go get him!" encouraged his master. "Chase that howling beast!"

Then the door was shut and the dog left outside, looking sadly toward the doorknob.

Coyote had retired to a safer distance. Now she came forward and whined. The Airedale took no notice. She whined again and began to sidle toward him, almost to prance. In a sudden rage, the dog rushed at her to drive

46

her away. She did not run. She met him nose to nose and would not move. Undecided, he managed to growl, then stalk away. Again she whined and played around him. He tried to growl but failed this time. He held his head high and was watching her. Instantly she tried to lure him away from the house, leaping around him playfully, nipping at his throat, pulling at his ear, but always moving toward the woods.

He walked toward her doubtfully. She capered and twisted and whined, then trotted away, but now he was trotting beside her. Together, they headed for the fields, the woods, the ravines of the Pennypack, the thickets that were so sunny all day, the glades of the quiet park, and the whole wonderful world that awaited their coming.

Two weeks were to go swiftly by before faithful Caesar was again to be seen at his home in the farm country, a different Caesar; alert, suspicious of humans, shy, and often with a faraway look in his brown eyes.

Chapter 6

"There's something unusual going on in our valley," commented Caesar's master to some of his friends. "I sent our Airedale out after a howling dog on our lawn and he didn't come home for weeks. When he did come home, he was as wild as a wolf; afraid of everything, even of us. He bolted his food and wanted to run away again, but I managed to tie him up. He'd lost his collar, however, and I had to get him a new one. And he'd grown a thicker coat of hair, just as if he'd stayed out in the cold and had to get more warmth somehow. It was all very, very strange!"

Mr. Horton heard of this and did not think it strange at all.

"What will happen next?" he wondered.

Another thing he learned interested him greatly. In recent weeks dogs had regularly upset garbage cans in the neighborhood. This had not happened before.

"There were two dogs," one man remarked. "One of them was an Airedale, the other was smaller, seemed sort of wild and stayed in the shadows just egging the first one on, so I did not get a good look at it."

"The coyote again," thought Mr. Horton. "Always that coyote!"

Several times Coyote came to call the Airedale. She howled but only once had any response. That time she heard the Airedale get a hard scolding. Soon, however, she had other things to think about, all of them hinging on the wonderful fact that she was going to have a litter of pups. Now, like the food-hoarding squirrels, she was burying all of the extra food she could find, hiding it deep enough that it would not spoil easily and would not be found by other animals and flies. At night she haunted the roads to pick up the creatures killed by hurrying motorists—opossums, cats, rabbits, anything that could be dug up later and used for food when hunting would be hard for her.

Once she had great luck. A doe had been run down by a car and left dead in the ditch. All that night, Coyote worked on the carcass, shearing off pieces of meat and carrying them to a safe burial place. The motorist reported the accident to the police, but when they arrived on the scene the next morning there was very little meat left; the poor doe was not to be wasted.

There was snow on the ground when the doe was killed, but when the police looked for tracks they found only those of what they thought was a small dog. Coyote had so cleverly managed her trips into the woods to bury the meat that the policemen could not follow her crisscross tracks. Grumbling, they buried the head, large bones, and other remains of the doe. A fine thing for Coyote. On the following night she dug these up and carried away all that she could.

Finding a suitable place for a den was not an easy

matter for her. She had to hide it from the crows; also she knew that it must be as far as possible from the haunts of man and so placed that she could go to it and from it without being seen. Instinctively she knew, too, that it must be on a slope where rain could not run or wash in, and, lastly, she knew that she alone could not dig a very big burrow; it must be a natural cave in the rocks or an enlarged burrow of a fox or woodchuck.

Every night she searched for a perfect place and at last found it. It was a hundred yards from the creek, where the police dogs had long ago tried to dig out a rabbit that sought safety in an old woodchuck burrow on a bushy hillside near Lorimer Park. That much settled, she started digging.

First she dug with her front feet until a pile of dirt had been accumulated under her; then she threw the pile out of the way by kicking backward with all four feet. The dirt was full of sand and so the work progressed fast, and soon the enlarged burrow turned nearly at right angles around a huge rock. This rock was what she prized most about the burrow; it would bother a digging enemy.

Every night she dug a little until she had gone fifteen feet into the side of the hill. Here was to be her room for the pups, well behind the boulder. Satisfied now, she stayed nearby to mount guard. Each day she went shorter distances around the country until, one night soon after the closing days of March, she did not feel equal to hunting at all and so retired to the bottom of the den.

Her puppies were born that night, six of them. They seemed very small and did not have their eyes open. She did not know exactly what they were, but she did know instinctively that they must be thoroughly licked, nursed, and kept from crawling away from her side. There was no bedding. They lay on the bare earth warmed by her furry body.

She stayed with them a day, then came out of the den to drink at the creek and dig up one of her caches of deer meat. The little ones snuggled together, moving only slightly and waiting for her return. For them it was just eat and sleep, then eat again.

The pups grew fast. In ten days their eyes, so tightly closed at birth, were opening, at first mere slits, then almost round. It was warm down there in the snug den, but almost completely dark. Days passed before the little wolves crawled nearer to the light and could see as well as scent and feel their mother whenever she came into the burrow to give them milk. Not always did she stay with them. More and more she preferred to take a stand at a short distance from the den where a mound beside a fallen tree gave her a good lookout post. When, however, the wind blew from her to the den, she changed her position to the other side, the better to smell an approaching enemy.

When the pups were a month old and beginning to be very active and strong, she threw up the contents of her stomach in front of them. This partly digested food, added to her now inadequate supply of milk, made the youngsters develop quickly. After another three weeks had passed, she stopped giving them milk and now regurgitated food regularly. They ate this ravenously, quarreling over it and bolting down all that they could. And at this point the mother began giving them some food freshly dug from her buried stores.

Every day the lively pups grew bolder and spent more time in the lighted entrance, where they could meet their mother sooner. It was not long before they were romping in the warm sunshine around the mouth of the den with plenty of room for their wrestling matches and a chance to see more of the world.

Four of the pups were larger and bolder than the other two. They were males. The mother treated them all alike, but they developed among themselves an understanding as to who could boss whom and get the first chance at any food. This depended as much on size and strength as on temperament. In their play they were very rough, but never rough enough to harm each other.

In the last days of May, Coyote commenced to bring her kill of young rabbits to the den. These the pups fell upon with delight and pulled at until each had a portion. She was still regurgitating other food for them, however, and working constantly to keep them fed. If she had been in Arizona with a coyote mate, he would have killed and brought much of the food to help with the pups. If it had not been for her caches, she, alone, might not have been able to raise the litter.

The time of plenty was beginning again. Young creatures were appearing everywhere along with the new growth of protecting leaves in the woods and fields. The young were uneducated in escaping the meat eaters and made easy game for Coyote. There were so many of them: woodchucks, rabbits, mice, and rats, snakes, frogs, and many kinds of birds and insects. Fruit, too, was important, especially strawberries, cherries, and mulberries.

Out in the farm country Mr. Horton had plowed, harrowed, and planted two fields. One contained corn, the

other all sorts of vegetables for the table, as well as water-melons and cantaloupes. One day in July he saw a surprising sight—the coyote sitting in the grass at a little distance, watching him work. She looked very wary but had no apparent fear. Mr. Horton, much perplexed, stood regarding her.

At length he said, "Hello there, girl."

At the sound of his voice the coyote stood up and quietly slipped into the wood. The next day, when he was again at work, he looked up to find seven coyotes regarding him. For a moment he was startled.

"Say, lady, that's quite a litter!" he said in greeting. Just as had happened before, the mother coyote turned back to the wood, this time followed quickly by her young.

Mr. Horton, much excited, hurried to his house and brought back pieces of ham and slices of bread. The coyotes were not in sight, but he dropped the food at the spot where they had gone into the wood. The next morning all of the food was gone, so he put out more. Of course he told Mrs. Horton and the boys about it, but, as always, asked them not to mention the coyotes to anyone. He was still afraid that some kind of trouble might result.

"The pups are now at least half the size of the mother," he told them enthusiastically. "Four are dark in color, one gray and one brown. They look like wolves but somehow also look like dogs. It's certainly interesting. Very, very interesting."

At the time Mr. Horton glimpsed them, they were in the short summer-hair stage. The baby wool was gone from the young ones, as well as the heavy fur from the

54

mother. The new coat grown by the pups showed much of the color that they would have through life.

The pups were never again to stay in the den. They followed their mother wherever she went, smelling everything, watching her hunt, and learning to hunt for themselves. And when the noon whistles blew loudly or an ambulance siren made the air throb, the whole family responded with a howling chorus. They could not resist it. The mother's howl was more musical than that of the youngsters. All of them yapped several times before the long howl commenced, and their teamwork and timing were so perfect that yaps and howls built up a long sequence of melody. Seven voices sounded like twice that number. People listened in awe, not understanding what had happened to bring so many "dogs" together each day.

It was now that unfortunate things began to happen. The wolf family, spreading out every night to cover the woods and fields, had disposed of the available food creatures and berries in a wide area. There were no more food caches to dig up. The hungry young wolves became unruly and split up in groups to hunt food, very soon learning to upset garbage cans at houses on all sides and to kill every chicken and duck they could find.

Four of them, going far afield, discovered a flock of sheep. They were afraid to molest them immediately, but at length on one fateful night, chased and killed two. The whole wolf family came together for a tremendous feast. The pack had worked silently and was not seen, but their tracks were everywhere. A great hullabaloo resulted. The owner of the sheep appealed to the dog-catcher and the police. No one thought of wolves; always it was stray dogs that were blamed. A war was started. Dog owners who had never bothered to secure licenses for their pets now rushed to register them and to keep them chained or housed.

Since the police, though interested, seemed unable to destroy the miscreant dogs, a group of sportsmen took over and organized an armed drive through the woodlands. They met where the sheep had been killed and combed the area, but found no dogs to shoot. No wonder, for at the first sign of trouble Coyote, sensing danger, had herded her brood into the far end of the park. She could convey fear to them, and when that happened they meekly followed her.

For nearly a week all stayed in or close to the park, picking up scraps left by picnickers, raiding garbage cans, and finishing off all the woodchucks and rabbits that remained there. Several times they were chased by dogs. From these they always ran at first, but if any small dog persisted in following, they turned on him. No small dog ever followed them twice. As yet, the youngsters had only their baby teeth, but these were very sharp.

Suddenly the pack came back to the farm land and extended its range in all directions. It found two large public dumping grounds that yielded much food, mixed in with newspapers, ashes, bottles, and tin cans. It located two more flocks of sheep, and also a herd of tame fallow deer enclosed behind high fences. Longingly the pack watched these. There might have been much trouble had they not discovered a melon patch and extensive apple and pear orchards with well-laden trees. The wind shook plenty of fruit to the ground, where it lay safely in the long grass until nosed out by the coyotes.

Chapter 7

MANY reports of damage to livestock were circulating in the Pennypack Valley. Two boys brought in a story about seeing three dark-colored dogs with reddish legs running together through the woods, the leader carrying a white Muscovy duck in its jaws. One man saw a grayish "dog" stalk and catch one of his leghorn hens that had wandered away from the yard. Another lost one of his Peking ducks nearly every morning, each somehow caught in the pond below his house. He saw no dogs and heard none, but there were tracks. And so it went, until the headstrong pups, losing some of the coyote wariness, showed themselves too openly in daylight. This led to a definite crusade against them, but still they were thought to be just dogs.

The mother lay low. She moved only at night now and stayed by herself, although she saw the pups somewhere every night in their rambles. If she could not catch a rabbit or a mouse or two, or find a dead bird, she ate fruit and even vegetables and caught grasshoppers that were partly numbed by the cold nights.

Meanwhile the pups managed to dig under fences and

kill two more sheep. They were becoming full grown, several inches taller than the mother and heavier in build. One female looked like Coyote but was yellower in color, the other female was bright gray with brown on her nose and front legs. The four males resembled the Airedale, for they had very dark backs and reddish legs.

The fight against the pack started this time with the setting of steel traps in the woods paths. In a community accustomed to trapping muskrats and an occasional raccoon or opossum, no one had any really large traps, which was a boon to the young wolves. On the first night, the pups bungled into four traps out of the many that were set. In each case the wolf was caught by one foot and firmly gripped by the steel jaws. Up into the air the youngster leaped with a yowl of surprise and pain, then it went wild with fear, leaping, clawing the ground, and biting the trap. Such were its weight and strength that in each case it pulled its foot free and galloped away, limping. Now it knew the danger in hidden traps, and so did the two remaining pups of the litter who had seen everything happen. That night the pack came together and howled dismally, not in the usual gay tone.

Mr. Horton heard the racket. He later heard the reports of the unsuccessful trapping and could not help being relieved, almost pleased. A meeting of sportsmen had been called to map out future strategy against these "dogs." Since Mr. Horton's conscience had been troubling him, now he eased it somewhat by telling the meeting the surprising news of the escape of the coyote.

"It's my fault," he concluded, "and I'm awfully sorry. What you are suffering from is a pack of six coyote-dogs, with my former pet leading them. She's just a wolf, of

58

course. I don't know the father, but I'm sure he's a dog. I have no sheep," he continued. "All I have suffered is a loss of tomatoes and watermelons. Those coy-dogs ate them in the garden just as they ripened and before I knew they should be gathered. Believe it or not, I'm sort of fond of that mother coyote. She's a great character. I'd catch her if I could and pen her up again for a pet—this time for keeps. It's the half-breed dogs, her pups, that I think you should catch."

For a minute there was complete silence, then ten men talked at once. A wolf! Of all things! And a litter of half-wolf pups raised and trained by a wolf! Now there was genuine enthusiasm over the prospect of catching them. Doing away with dogs had never been popular, but wolves or half wolves—well, that was different. Oddly enough, no one seemed to bear a grudge against Mr. Horton.

It ended with one of the men, Jeremy Jones, who trapped and hunted occasionally, being appointed leader, empowered to buy much larger steel traps, to organize hunting groups, to use hounds for tracking or anything else he thought advisable, barring poison. All agreed that poison was too much of a danger to more than just the wolves.

Jeremy was a short, stocky man of middle age. He enjoyed nothing as much as poking around the woods, looking at Nature in all its forms. And he knew a great deal about the creek and its bush-covered banks. He fished there all summer. After buying a dozen large steel traps, he spent a whole day in looking for wolf tracks and trying to find the pack's principal paths through the woodlands. He wore dark gray clothes that merged with the color of tree trunks, and he moved so slowly that he was able to slip up on squirrels and many other woods creatures without alarming them far ahead, but he was not able to come near the wolves. They spotted him and retreated into Lorimer Park.

He found their fresh tracks, however, and knew then that the park area was their stronghold and that the best place to trap them would be in the paths they followed in going to and from the parks. Here he would set all of his traps.

First, Jeremy boiled the traps in wood ashes and lye to rid them of human scent and the rust smell, then he carried them to the woods with clean canvas gloves and planted them in sets of two where tracks showed the path that the wolves normally traveled. Each trap was set in a shallow bed dug with a trowel. The bed brought the jaws of the trap slightly below the level of the path. Between the jaws on top of the trap's pan he placed waxed paper to keep the dirt that he sifted over the set from getting under the pan and preventing the weight of an animal from tripping it. When he was through, the trap was invisible. The short chain and wire attached to it were buried and the wire fastened around a nearby tree.

To make the set perfect, he placed some dead branches across the path to block it except where the traps were placed, and in front of each trap he propped a twig over which the wolf should step and get his foot exactly in the trap. He himself avoided walking in the path.

Jeremy's home was not far from the woods and in the night he heard howling.

"I've got one!" he thought joyfully. In the early morning he hurried out, armed with a .22-caliber rifle, and he

found a coyote-dog in the very first set, one of the dark-colored males. The twenty-five pound animal leaped about, then sullenly regarded him. All around it the earth was clawed up. Jeremy was elated. He felt no compunction in firing the fatal bullet.

He hastened to the next set. Here was another dark-colored male, caught in two traps! Jeremy finished this one and felt mighty proud. In the third set he had an opossum. In the fourth a lively black skunk with white on its forehead, what the furriers called a valuable star black. He shot the skunk and passed on quickly ahead of the fumes. There was nothing in the next set and only an old gray squirrel in the last. Now he had before him the task of disposing of the skunk, burying the larger animals, too, and resetting the traps.

While he was digging, an ambulance passed down the pike a few hundred yards away. Its siren was going full blast.

"Now," thought Jeremy, "the wolves will howl." And sure enough, a great babel of voices rose from across the ravine. "That must mean the mother has brought them together," he thought, "and will try to keep them out of trouble." He was right in his guess.

As soon as the first pup had been caught in the trap the night before and started howling, the old coyote came to him. A pup that had been with him rushed for the park and was caught in another set almost immediately. The mother circled both of the struggling young ones several times, calling to them, but finally she sensed that she could not help them. Still she hung around and in her anxiety almost got caught in a set that was planted in another path. Luck was with her, however, for she felt the trap's pan drop and jumped before the jaws bit. Now in great alarm she gave a gruff call and brought the remaining four pups, all of them chastened by their brothers' outcry. They were so wrought up that they could not help howling when they heard the siren.

A heavy rain that afternoon drove the wolves to a thicket of young pines that shed much of the water in the manner of an umbrella. The rain was hard enough to wash mud into the trap sets and spoil Jeremy's careful work of the morning, and it made the air so full of moisture that fog hung over the ground. Through this the moon cast a weird glow. Such perfect weather for stalking came only occasionally, so that evening Coyote made the most of it. She led the pups to the lawn of house after house and, under cover of the fog, chased the rabbits almost in the shadow of the houses.

The pack fanned out and swept across the lawns. The surprised rabbits bolted for the nearest cover, trying to get past the line of eager wolves. There was just enough light to give perfect visibility for the work. Three rabbits and one barn rat were caught in the silent, quick drives.

The pups, a bit unruly, tried to catch a Maltese cat, which, however, managed to climb to safety up a tree. At a call from their mother, they turned away to follow her behind a barn where two tall persimmon trees were loaded with ripening fruit. That night two heavy old opossums were in these trees, climbing to the tips of the limbs to reach the best persimmons. They clumsily shook down many that the wolves could pick up below, bolting them down seeds and all.

Back of the barn was a manure pile in which the farmer had buried two scrawny chickens that had died of old age or disease. These Coyote quickly scented and dug up, the young wolves joining in the feast. The fact that the meat was very high from having been in the manure for nearly a week did not in the least dim its flavor. Feathers and bones went with it.

Now Coyote loped to a remote lawn where she had never been before. Again the pack fanned out. Two rabbits leaped up ahead. The pups were after these, when they ran full tilt into a dog's runway. The big police dog that once had nearly killed Coyote in her pen was fastened by a chain to a long overhead wire that enabled him to run backward and forward for exercise.

When the pack of coyotes suddenly descended on the

place, the big dog charged out of his box with fierce barking. The wolves scattered in alarm. In his fury the dog broke the chain at his collar and dashed after them. He picked out the smallest, the gray female, and followed her at full speed, gaining at every leap. She ran her fastest but was not old enough to outdistance this much larger animal, which was, indeed, cousin to the European wolves. Suddenly he was upon her, but she dodged. Again he overtook her, but this time at his flank ran another wolf trying to lure him away. With a roar, he turned.

Then it was really a race. Coyote could run fully as fast as he could, and she was deliberately taking him away from her litter. They went through a big field and ran down a country lane. They crossed the hard-surfaced pike and were again tearing over lawns. The dog was not barking now; he was saving his breath. And he was game. Above everything else he meant to catch the wolf, and nothing would stop him.

Coyote was fully aware of her danger. If she tripped or were cornered, she was sure to be caught. Feeling hampered by the load of food in her stomach, she disgorged it. Now she was running in almost a straight line as if with a definite goal. Her long tail was dragging and she was tiring just enough to worry her. Suddenly she turned sharply to the right, then to the left, following a pathway. The dog gained by cutting straight across. Again she did the same thing and the dog again cut across, but this time with a shrill yelp of pain. When she continued to make turns, he dropped behind and quit the race.

She ran a short distance and looked back. The dog was

lying down. All around were tin cans and bottles, papers and ashes. They were in the town's dump, and broken glass had badly cut two of the heavy dog's feet when he dashed across corners instead of following the rambling pathway. Coyote did not gloat. She just turned away, much relieved because the dog did not follow. And so at length she had her revenge, but who can say that she knew the dog would be injured? From recent visits, however, she did know that here was a place where scent did not lie well and where it might be possible to dodge an enemy among the heaps of debris.

Coyote loped back to find her pups. The police dog lay for some time licking his wounds, then he bravely bore the pain of walking and slowly hobbled home, hating the coyote more than ever.

Chapter 8

JEREMY stood in a wood bordering the Pennypack Creek, looking at the water's current strain around some big rocks. Several days had passed since the heavy rain, but the water still was high and slightly muddy. There were no insects to make the chub and sunfish rise to the surface, frogs and turtles were already in the mud hibernating, and water snakes had crawled far down among rocks that men had dumped at bends to prevent erosion by floods. As usual, Jeremy was thinking very hard.

"The third day of the shooting season and gunners everywhere. Three weeks before I dare reset traps in the paths. Why not get together at least ten hunters and drive the woodlands? I could station five men with guns along the edge of Lorimer Park and have five or more without guns walk through both parks and drive the coyotes out. I doubt whether the animals will run into the fields or lawns during daylight. They'll follow the bushes and timber. Someone will get a chance for shots. It can't fail! And how could the park guards object to men just walking in the park for the drive? Anyway, the guards don't like wolves!"

And on that basis Jeremy organized a big hunt for the following Saturday, a hunt that he thought would exterminate the coyote pack. Only one person, Chris Morgan, tried to dissuade him, for he was a friend to all wild things. When Jeremy explained his plan, this man objected vehemently. He and Jeremy had a bitter altercation. Finally Chris Morgan strode out of the room.

Coyote had rushed her four young ones into the parks as soon as the gunshots announced the beginning of the hunting season. At night they came out to range the fields for wounded and dead game, then hurried back to the sanctuary. When the fateful Saturday came, they were bedded on a brush-covered bank well within the park's borders, and they could see in every direction. This was the time of day when they loafed, licked paws, and put all their fur in order.

When the men who were to make the drive lined up and started to march, two deer were disturbed. They jumped up from their beds and ran along the bank of the creek, passing below the bushes where the wolves rested. That was enough warning to make Coyote suspicious. She soon heard the men approaching in their long line. Now she knew that some new kind of danger was afoot. Two gray squirrels and a rabbit dashed past her to add to her fears. Crows were cawing an alarm.

Coyote loped to the waiting pups. She stood among them, listening and sniffing the breeze. All were on their feet. She heard crows cawing in several directions, telling of danger, and she knew that gunners would be in the fields as usual, perhaps everywhere, except in the park. The pups, thoroughly uneasy, walked about and wanted to bolt. A rabbit hopped past, quickening his pace when he saw some of the pack. The wolves heard twigs snap and canvas clothing rub loudly against bushes and briers.

Still Coyote was undecided what to do. She feared to leave the park in spite of the advancing line of men. Around her was dense underbrush, mostly laurel with high briers among the bushes. The wolves could easily slip underneath such thick cover, but a man could scarcely tear his way through it unless he went down on hands and knees. Coyote made up her mind; she would remain hidden there. Passing from pup to pup, she gained their attention, then she crouched flat on the ground, head down, like a rabbit in its bed. The pups understood and did likewise.

The line of men came slowly nearer, making more and more noise. They thumped their feet awkwardly as they walked and they exclaimed whenever a brier pricked a hand or knee. The wolves hugged the ground without moving, but they were almost in terror. Men had never been able to come so close before. And they were coming nearer every moment. From the corners of their eyes, the pups watched their mother, and tensed their muscles for a dash away. Nearer and nearer came the men, so loud now in their advance that there was constant crashing. The wolves could glimpse their forms among the trees.

At the laurel thicket two of the men began to break their way in. They were only a dozen yards from the wolves. Coyote flattened herself even more, just as she had done in the pigeon pen to escape notice. But the men were hesitating. Presently they decided to go around the prickly thicket, one on each side beating bushes with a stick. They were very close to the wolves.

One of the men fell and pitched down flat on his stomach with such a crash that one of the pups could not stand the strain and bolted. It was one of the two males. He dashed away in the direction that the drivers wanted him to go. Suddenly there was a shot, then two more shots. The remaining coyotes never saw him again. Now there were three pups and the mother.

The big drive ended with the death of only one coyote-dog, but it was declared a success. Everyone wondered what had become of the other wolves, but no one could give a satisfactory answer. Jeremy, however, pussyfooting through the bushes afterward, accurately guessed the procedure of the wolves. That evening he brought together some of his friends and arranged a hunt with hounds to drive out the wolves and give the gunners a better chance.

The big question was where to get hounds that would trail coyotes. Jeremy solved this by writing the various dealers around the country. One of them had two foxhounds that in the company of greyhounds had chased coyotes for a year on a Western ranch. They were old but good, the man claimed. Add a few young hounds to run with these and you had a fine combination! Jeremy agreed and hired the dealer to manage a hunt. Again he had angry opposition from Chris Morgan but did not heed it.

By this time the three coyote pups had succeeded in digging under the wire fence that contained the herd of tame fallow deer, killing two of them, one a doe, the other a buck. In the eyes of the community that was the "last straw," especially as the remaining deer had broken down the fence in their wild attempt to escape the wolves and now were ranging all around the farm land. The white-tailed deer were hard enough on gardens without having any help from the half-tame fallows.

Jeremy begged the owner of the two deer that were killed to leave the carcasses lying exactly where they were found. These he thought would keep the wolves coming back to the spot every night. Again he mustered a small army of gunners. This time it was planned to have the men line up before dawn along the wooded boundary of the park and thus prevent the wolves from going there ahead of the hunt. The hounds would be released at the pen of the fallow deer when there was enough light, and would be made to range the woodland on all sides until they struck a fresh trail. It all sounded perfect.

Jeremy himself attended to motoring the gunners as far as the edge of Lorimer Park and placing them thirty yards apart. Then he brought the hounds and their owner to the deer pen. In the early light of a cold morning, with frost all over the meadows, it was spooky enough to please anyone. In all there were six hounds, full of excitement. They bayed and growled at each other in the car, but when they were released they ran at once to the deer carcasses and began to eat vension. Jeremy was mad, the dealer was equally mad, and the hounds were quickly chased out of the pen. Now officially the hunt was supposed to have begun, but the hounds, robbed of the dead deer breakfast, started after the live fallow deer in the fields and woods. That meant much chasing, scolding, and delay.

70

"It's those young dogs that make the trouble," growled their owner. He managed to catch and put all four on leash so that the two older hounds could work without being distracted. And work they did. It was not long before they were baying in the woods, trying to follow tracks that seemed to puzzle them. Jeremy and their owner attempted to see what kind of animal they were following. In the dry leaves this was difficult.

"I believe it's a wolf!" yelled Jeremy. "I see no hoof marks such as a deer would make."

"Let's go, boys!" shouted the owner encouragingly.

For a short time the hounds poked along, only occasionally baying. Then things changed. They started a wild clamor and fairly rushed through the woods. The owner was dancing with excitement. He unleashed the young hounds, who were straining to be free.

"Yippee!" he shouted. "We've got one going! He won't get away from these hounds! Which direction are the guns?"

"In the opposite direction from where we are headed."

"That's bad!" muttered the owner. "We don't want to cross any automobile roads before someone gets a shot. Hounds get killed on roads!"

But the direction did not change. Whatever was ahead of the hounds was leading them away from the woods and into the built-up area at high speed. Now they were going across lawns and paved streets, the six bunched together. Boys were shouting and whistling, dogs barking, girls screaming, autos honking. No one seemed to know what was going on. It was wild bedlam.

"Mad dog!" yelled someone. "Look out! Police! Police!"

71

In the rear Jeremy and the owner followed as best they could in a car they had borrowed from a farmer.

"Never saw anything like this!" panted the owner. "There hasn't been a check. It's full speed all the time. And on the streets—anywhere. It's crazy. It can't last like this!" But last it did. They went around half the town, then across country to the railroad, then beside the railroad for a mile, then in a half-circle to another town.

Far in the rear, but keeping on the track of the chase by the help of excited people along the way, came Jeremy and the owner, bumping along and pushing the farmer's old car to its best. They were almost bounced to pieces, but they would not give up.

"This," said the owner, "is the world's greatest hunt!"

"We're making history!" breathed Jeremy.

At a crossroad they found one of the two older hounds lying stretched out as if dead. But he was not dead—he was completely tired out. They picked him up and put him in the rear of the car. A short distance farther they found the second old hound and put him with the first. The four younger ones were still running ahead.

"Aren't we headed back?" asked the owner.

"We sure are! Straight for the park!"

"Thank goodness!" muttered the owner. "I'm about done in just riding the bumps! This is terrific! A coyote is a good runner, but this one is the champ of them all. I wouldn't have missed this for anything!"

"Isn't it great! We'll have something to tell our children and our children's children!"

"I haven't any children," growled the owner.

"Oh well, skip it. We'll hear a shot any moment now."

They were on a path that led to the park. Trees hemmed them in and the car scraped bushes. Ahead the hounds bayed hoarsely as they ran.

"The guns can't be far," Jeremy began hopefully. "Any second now we'll have that wolf—any second."

Suddenly they rounded a corner and came almost on top of the first gunner, who had left his stand and was in the path. Beyond him they saw a cluster of men. They were holding the hounds by the collars. Their guns were on the ground or leaning against trees.

Jeremy put on the brakes so hard he almost sent the owner through the windshield.

"Where's the wolf?" he gasped. There was no reply.

"Didn't you see him? Why didn't you shoot? Did he get into the park?"

"No, and he didn't get into the park," answered one of the gunners. "And we didn't want to shoot him."

"But why, why?"

"Well," continued the man, "we would have liked to shoot him but we couldn't."

"Again, I ask why?" pleaded Jeremy.

"There are two pretty good reasons," drawled the man. "First of all, he was riding a motorcycle and, second, he was waving a flag on a stick, so we wouldn't mistake him for a wolf."

"What!" gasped Jeremy. "What!"

"Yes, and he was dragging a bag full of trapper's fox scent strengthened with anise seed. You should have seen the happy expression on the hounds when they followed it!"

"I'll consider lending you my shooting iron if you want

to take a crack at him," continued the man pleasantly. "You look mad enough to do almost anything right now."

But at first Jeremy was so exasperated that he was speechless. Finally he managed to ask, "Was it that fellow, Chris Morgan?"

"I think that's still his name," was the reply. "Speaking seriously, he pulled quite a humorous stunt."

Then at last Jeremy leaned back his head and actually began to laugh. It was very mirthless and dry, but it was a laugh.

The owner, pretending to speak to himself, said, "I can scarcely wait to tell my children's children!"

Chapter 9

JEREMY bore up well under the teasing handed him by his friends. It surprised him to find how far and wide the story of the wolf hunt had spread. But now he had a new idea. He would build a small platform hidden up in a tree near the main path in the woods and there lie in wait with his gun for the wolves to pass. The wolves then would not scent him or see him, and he would have a fine view over the underbrush.

The gunning season had ended and mid-December had brought some light snow and low temperatures. The scrub oaks still bore their dead leaves, but the woods in most places were bare and bleak. Jeremy's tree stand, firmly nailed between the trunk of an oak and two of its limbs, could be reached by a rope ladder nearly twenty feet long.

By this time he had a calendar on which were marked the days when the wolves in their hunting cycle around the country would be most likely to use the path he would guard. Dressed so warmly that he could scarcely walk, he took his stand on a promising day when snow was still on the ground and a full moon would help him

75

to see after the sun had set. He climbed the shaky ladder at three o'clock and from that moment never ceased to scan the surrounding woods.

It was a day when all of the wild creatures were feeding. Those that were left by the gunners and predators such as the coyotes were full grown now. The winter birds were everywhere; he saw downy woodpeckers, cardinals, juncos, field sparrows, chickadees, crows, and two red-tailed hawks. Several gray squirrels went past in long leaps, one of them carrying a hickory nut held by his teeth.

Just after the sun set, a great horned owl hooted far away, and was answered very soon by his mate. The interchange of loud hoots interested Jeremy greatly. Then slowly, timidly a doe walked along the path. She was in winter gray and fitted so well into the background of tree trunks that Jeremy did not see her until she was close. A few moments later a smaller doe appeared, stepping almost in the tracks of the first and watching ahead to note whether anything frightened the leader.

Jeremy stayed very still. The deer did not detect him. Presently he saw a brown rabbit hop out of a thicket and go from one small seedling to another, nipping off all of them so that when they lay on the snow the buds could easily be eaten. The rabbit seemed almost like a shadow. Again the horned owls hooted, and presently a screech owl whinnied softly. The woods even on winter nights were full of life. Jeremy felt cramped and cold but dared not move.

"Now is the time!" he thought, straining his eyes to see in the moonlight.

When the wolves came, he was caught by surprise.

Two of them approached so stealthily that they were within a few yards, almost beside his tree. There they stopped as if extremely suspicious. Jeremy knew that if he moved at all they would see him and bolt. He crouched with fast-beating heart, waiting for them to go farther away.

There was a whine from somewhere in front. Instantly the two wolves that were so close turned and slipped back through the bushes. Jeremy threw up his gun, aimed, and fired at the one to the right. In the stillness of the night the explosion sounded terrific.

Now Jeremy clambered down the ladder, turned on a flashlight, and examined the snow where the wolves had last been seen. He found where their feet had torn long scars when they leaped from the explosion, and he found where the pellets he fired had torn into the bushes. With sinking spirits he walked farther, sure that he had missed. But ahead was a brown object on the snow. He hurried to it and shone his light on a dead brown coyote-dog female. Greatly surprised, he stood looking at it, admiring the heavy fur.

"Only that old coyote and two of her pups left," was his thought. Then he lifted the dead wolf by her hind legs and started through the woods toward his car at the pike. No use to wait for another shot in that spot. But one thing puzzled him: "How did the old coyote know I was there?" he mused. "She evidently whined a warning."

Coyote, ever watchful, had seen the platform and the crouching lump. She stood in the bushes studying them until sure that they meant danger, then gave her warning. Other animals had not looked up in the trees for possible enemies because no motion caught their attention.

She and the two remaining young ones made a wide detour and by chance came upon a white fallow deer at the edge of the farm land. The deer bolted along the side of the wood in its jerky jumps and made such an enticing target for a chase that the pups at once started after it. Both quickly outran it. They sprang for its hind legs several times and eventually tripped it. Flat on the ground, the buck did not have a chance.

While the pups chewed and ate, Coyote stood guard. She was too shaken by the events of the evening to relax. When the young ones sprawled on the ground, their stomachs almost too full to let them travel, she bolted down a few mouthfuls of venison, then began to circle to assure herself that no man was sneaking up on them.

It was then that a strange thing happened; she saw a large animal approaching and almost at the same moment scented dog. The dog caught sight of her and stopped in his tracks. Then the two stood like statues regarding each other from a distance. The dog moved first. He strode forward, stiff-legged and full of formality. She waited. By this time she had recognized him: the Airedale, her devoted companion of the previous winter.

He got no farther. From the edge of the wood came the two pups to intercept him; they were trotting and they were full of curiosity. They felt animosity, too, because this dog was nearing their kill. The gray female was the first to come close, and almost at once her manner softened. Had the dog been a female like herself, jealousy would have increased the tension. It was very different with her brother. He was almost the same height as the Airedale and felt himself important enough to dispute the right of another male to come into his territory and to his kill.

The two, looking much alike, and acting alike, walked around each other. They were ready for trouble, but neither wanted to start it. The Airedale was becoming annoyed because the other did not seem satisfied with the usual introduction formalities. He growled. His son growled back. They walked side by side, glaring at each other sideways. Then they stood still. Now was when the younger animal should have backed away, acknowledging the other's rights and showing his own good nature. But the wolf was headstrong as well as young and he sprang at Caesar.

The fight was furious. At first it was noisy with growls and yelps. Then it was grimly silent. The wolf would bite and run, then dash back and try to bite again. Twice they rose together on hind legs and fiercely bit at each other's heads, only to fall to the ground and break away. That was when the young wolf realized that fighting a battle singlehanded against a powerful adversary was no fun. He backed away. He missed the help his brothers had always given him.

As for the Airedale, he was not inclined to push for more. He was good-natured and had simply been defending himself. Now he sat on his haunches and shook his head sorrowfully to lighten the pain in a cut ear and a bitten lip. For a minute or two, all four sat on the moonlit snow, the three wolves looking watchfully at the dog and the dog, in his turn, regarding them while he rested.

Presently Coyote came forward and stood so close to Caesar that she and he could touch noses. They were

getting acquainted again. Then she leaned forward and licked his bleeding ear. Once started, she licked it thoroughly and matted the hair over the wound. The pups took their cue from her and advanced to sniff, now showing no hostility. All at once everything had become friendly.

When at length the wolves started for the parks, Caesar tagged along behind them but found their pace too much for him. He dropped back, then stopped and soon turned around. The spirit of the wild was not in his veins. He was a house dog and little more. His hunting with the beagle had been a kind of escapade that ended when the beagle was run over by an automobile. True, Coyote had beguiled him into turning wolf for a time and he had not forgotten her. Had his master not kept him from straying, he would have gone into the woods to search for her many times.

Caesar traipsed quietly home and scratched on the front door. He was not particularly happy over his reception by the wolves, and he would need to forget this before he ran away again to join them. No one let him into the house at once, but later quite a fuss was made over his condition. He felt himself a hero.

No one made any fuss over Coyote; she was on her own and an outcast, and part of the world had pledged itself against her. As if to show her disregard for this, she joined the pups on the following night in pulling down another fallow deer. Few people seemed to care much about this deer, but two nights later the wolves raided a henroost and fought a battle with two dogs. The owner braved pneumonia, ran out in his nightshirt, and shot the male pup, which was the only one he saw in the darkness.

The remnant of the wolf pack, Coyote and her beautiful gray-coated daughter, loped back to the park. And that was when Jeremy was encouraged to set more traps.

Coyote and her daughter showed great affection for each other. Now that the daughter was the only one left of the young ones, she and her mother romped and played together after the hunting. They were inseparable. Coyote increased their range as far as the wide Delaware River in the east and the Neshaminy Creek in the north; miles of woods and fields, gardens and golf courses, a happy hunting ground indeed. Only occasionally did the two come to their old range, the park, and to the woods and fields near Mr. Horton's home.

Therefore, Jeremy's traps had small chance of success, even though some were baited with meat and others with coyote scent he had purchased. On one morning, however, he had a disagreeable surprise. In one of the traps, firmly held by a front foot, was a police dog, one of a roving pair. At the first glance Jeremy thought that he had a wolf, then his heart sank when he saw a black collar.

The little man approached guardedly to try to release the dog and was met with warning growls. The dog did not trust him and would not allow him to come near. Jeremy tried again and again, then gave it up. Returning home, he telephoned his closest neighbor, Mr. Horton, who recognized the dog when he was told that it wore a black collar. Jeremy, with plenty of misgivings, telephoned the owner and led him out to the poor dog. Some time elapsed before the nervous animal would let even his master work on the trap. It was a nerve-racking ordeal

83

and the owner was anything but happy. He said some rather cutting things to Jeremy. Eventually the foot was freed; the dog limped away, and Jeremy made a vow: never again would he be so foolish as to set wolf traps in the Pennypack Valley.

Chapter 10

SNOW was deep on the ground in late January, the creek was frozen over, and everything inhospitable, but Coyote was happy. This was the only place like a home she had. The hooting of the owls soothed her at night, and in the woods the tracks of the white-tailed deer and other wild creatures seemed the same as always. She wandered about, studying the paths, the thickets, the fields, and many more familiar places. The young one trailed along, but without the same enthusiasm.

Late one night, Coyote, sitting on her haunches near the creek, raised her nose and howled. She howled again and again. And the young one howled with her. As usual, dogs near and far barked and yapped in sympathy. Then Coyote started toward the farm country and, as once before, she headed for Caesar's home behind the big lawn. Here she howled once more and with such a lonesome quaver that Caesar answered dolefully from behind the locked doors of the house and tried his best to break out.

The household was aroused, and Caesar's owner came downstairs to quiet him. But this proved impossible. Well-trained, gentlemanly Caesar was all at once a changed animal. He wanted to get out, and he began to scratch and bite the kitchen door. In vain his owner scolded him. Whenever the dog seemed to have calmed down, the coyote howled. That set him to running about and chewing the door some more. At length his owner gave up.

"All right," he said, "if you want to be a fool and get eaten up by the wolves, get out of here! It will serve you right!" He opened the kitchen door. Caesar sprang out and into the night. It was more than a week later that he returned, this time just as shy and nervous as the year before.

On April Fools' Day, Coyote descended into her old den near Lorimer Park and bore five little wolves. They resembled the first litter so closely that anyone would have known they had the same father. Coyote had found a dead deer near the creek from which she had secured meat for the caches that now served her well. And when the young ones began to come out of the den for their play in the gentle days and warm sun of spring, the female pup of the previous litter helped Coyote to feed them with animals she caught.

April was the month in which the woodchucks came forth, sought mates, and migrated from the winter dens in the woods to field dens for the summer feeding. They were thin, almost scrawny, from their long winter sleep, but they were worth catching and both coyotes worked on them every day. They caught rabbits at night, woodchucks and gray squirrels in the daytime, and smaller creatures at any time.

This was the month when the boy scouts started their hikes and games in and around the parks. This year they

had a particularly energetic scoutmaster who kept them busy whenever they were not in school. One thing he insisted on was that they know every acre in the area and what trees, bushes, and plants it bore. One day three of the boys went to a knoll not previously covered, and to their surprise found Coyote's den.

None of them knew what was in the den. They stood around the entrance and made wild guesses. But all at once Coyote came trotting past in the bushes to entice them away, and the den was explained. In great excitement, they ran to tell the scoutmaster.

Coyote was badly frightened. She circled, then ran to

the burrow and called the pups. The first one that appeared she seized by the neck and began to carry away from danger. She loped through the woods without any definite idea of where to take her burden until she remembered a place she had once carefully examined as a possible den. It was a mass of stones and crumbling walls, the ruins of a house that had burned down years before. It stood at the edge of the woodland directly behind Mr. Horton's fields. Among the stones were two woodchuck burrows that could be enlarged, and into one of these she pushed the pup, who by this time was almost strangled by her hold. After looking about for danger and seeing none she started back to the den to move more pups.

Cautiously approaching the knoll, she heard voices. Her worst fears were realized, for now the den was surrounded by humans. Some were scouts, others workmen from the pike. In vain she circled through the brush to lure them from the den. Twice she barked at a distance, but no one saw her or noticed her calls, so intent were they on digging. She circled until the crowd left the spot.

When the voices had died away, Coyote approached the den with utmost care lest there be an ambush or trap. But the knoll was deserted and bare. A gaping hole showed where the snug burrow had been.

Coyote examined every inch of the ground. She dug here and there in the fresh earth, but all in vain, for the pups were gone. She could not know that they were to be given care and a home in a zoo. That night she was still wandering around the woodland, occasionally giving a short howl. At first the other coyote came with her, but after a time she left to search for food. Once more alone, Coyote soon stopped searching and ran all of the way to the ruins of the old house and her sole remaining pup. Finding him crouching miserably in the mouth of the woodchuck burrow, she hauled him out and dropped down beside him so that he could warm himself against her body and feed.

The remainder of the night and the early morning she spent in digging down deeper and deeper among the rocks until she had enlarged the slanting burrow to a length of nearly a dozen feet, ending it with the room where the pup could lie beyond the reach of the outside cold. It was rough, but it would do. Then she nursed him and left him curled up there alone while she mounted guard near the burrow's mouth. On a slab of stone on top of a rock pile a few feet above the ground and partly hidden by bushes, she relaxed at last and licked her tired feet. Around her were crumbling walls, bushes, briers and many vines, behind these the edge of the woodland. In front were two small fields, then the gardens of Mr. Horton's home.

Nothing disturbing happened all morning. Migrating birds drifted by, some far overhead, others very low, a few alighting on the ruins. Coyote's enemies, the crows, were busy somewhere else in the woods. The afternoon, however, was different. Not long after the sun had passed its height for the day there was the sound of voices. They came closer. Coyote slipped from her slab and circled behind the ruins for a safer look. Coming toward her through the field were a woman and a little girl.

Fear for a few moments swept over the wolf, but since women and small children had never done her harm, and she had seen many in the park, she was undecided just what to do. When close to the ruins, the little girl ran forward and began to climb on the rock piles in a kind of childish game. Her nurse sat down on a stone and read a book.

Coyote sat on her haunches in the bushes, watching and worrying. Presently the little girl ran to the nurse and extracted a paper bag from a parcel the woman had been carrying. Out of this the child pulled, one by one, a sandwich, two cookies, and an apple. She nibbled sparingly and threw the remainders away. The breeze being right, the wolf could smell these.

When the sun was on such a slant that it was no longer pleasantly warm, the woman and the little girl departed hand in hand through the fields. Then Coyote at once came forward and ate the scraps left by the child. Back on her slab she looked in all directions, trying to satisfy herself that the place was safe for the young one in the burrow. Later she went on a tour of the ruins. The fact that other wild creatures lived there made her feel more secure. The rock piles seemed to be a haven for rabbits, opossums, and skunks; their smell was everywhere.

That night she saw a mother skunk come out of the second old woodchuck burrow and wander into the fields in search of bumblebee nests and meadow mice. The skunk was not afraid for herself but kept looking back to make sure that her eight young in the burrow would not be harmed. An opossum crouched for some time on a rock pile, trying to decide whether the coyote was going to prove dangerous. Satisfied at length, she climbed down and shuffled off, taking care not to jar the eleven young ones she was carrying in the furry pouch under her body.

Coyote at length decided that for the present all was

well. Away she loped in the light of the stars to give the knoll near the park border one more look-over before relinquishing hope and never visiting the unlucky place again. On the way back she was joined by her grown young one. Near the new den this young one stopped and then trotted away. She seemed to have lost interest in staying with her mother. Coyote looked after her and whined. The young one did not stop. If she thought that now she could take care of herself, she was very wrong. On the following evening, when hunger dulled her caution, she raided a chicken coop and in such a stupid way that the owner, after hearing the squawking, had time to come downstairs with a flashlight and his gun. He could not see her, but his flashlight was reflected in her eyes, which she had not turned away. At once he fired and with deadly aim. And so Coyote was all alone with her one young pup. The trouble she had had in raising a litter during the year before went for naught. She wondered why she did not see the gray daughter any more, and she missed her.

Now Coyote could catch the full-grown rabbits only by stalking them alone, which was a difficult process. First she quartered a field or wood patch until she scented fresh rabbit tracks. She followed with utmost stealth until by sight, scent, or sound she located a feeding rabbit. After that, she crawled upwind to within leaping distance, waited for the rabbit to bend down for a bite of clover or whatever he was eating, then sprang upon him and seized him so firmly with her teeth that he could not kick loose.

Her usual attack on a woodchuck was very different.

Since the home and retreat of a formidable chuck was one of his several burrows, and since he fed in daylight, she hid herself in the morning close to a burrow that she knew by the strong scent a chuck was using. Whether male or female, old or young, the chuck would act in the same way. First he would raise his head to the level of the ground around the burrow's mouth, and, his head being flat, his protruding eyes could then see all around. After a minute or more he would come up higher and soon be ready to make his way to clover or other food patch.

It was no easy matter for the hungry coyote to delay until the chuck had gone a yard or two from the hole before she made her dash, but he could turn and go down his burrow in a flash if given the chance. And if her jaws did not catch him by the neck close to his head, his long, dangerous teeth would reach her. Coyote handled a big old chuck with caution. She dashed and seized him wherever she could get a quick hold, and then she tried to throw him away from the burrow. He would not dare turn his back to her, so would crouch facing her and try to edge closer to the burrow, meanwhile growling, clicking his jaws, and sometimes whistling shrilly as he struck at her with teeth bared.

She would leap this way and that until she saw a good chance to seize him by the neck and throw him flat on the ground. After that she would not let go until his kicking ceased. The hide was so tough that she always carried or dragged a chuck to a thicket or other safe place to eat him leisurely. Those that weighed more than five or six pounds she could not finish entirely, preferring to bury the extra meat for another day. Sometimes she had to bury more than half an old male chuck.

In late May or June the young chucks were driven forth from the burrow to find one of their own. Coyote caught them easily. These young ones would fight, but as their main concern was finding enough food to keep their stomachs full, they often wandered far from any protective hole.

Chapter 11

Every sunny day the nurse and the little girl went to the old ruins. And every day Coyote picked up food scraps after they had left. Both she and the pup, now a fast-growing, skinny little fellow, were becoming accustomed to their visits, until they reached a point where there seemed to be no sense in going into hiding. The little girl was the first to see the pup. It was watching her from the entrance of the burrow. The little girl was delighted to have found such a pretty puppy and, of course, tried to come nearer and feed it. The pup retreated but came out again as soon as the child moved away. This happened several times and ended in the pup's seizing a piece of sandwich left for him.

Next day the pup came out when the child arrived. He wanted more sandwich. Meanwhile the mother watched from her slab and did not move. But just as soon as the nurse saw what was going on and hurried to the little girl, the coyotes vanished. That evening the nurse reported the matter to her employers, who certainly knew something about wolves because they were Mr. and Mrs. Horton. Their two boys heard it, too, and were

full of curiosity. All turned out on the following morning to have a look.

Mr. Horton was wise enough to keep well away from
the burrow and from a distance see enough to be fairly
sure that there were only one pup and an older coyote,
its mother, no doubt his sons' onetime pet, so long lost to
them. He threw some breakfast scraps on the ground,
then herded the others away. The nurse and his little
girl were to come there in the afternoon as usual. And
their coming somehow reassured Coyote and kept her
from moving the pup a second time.

The little fellow really was growing now that his
mother was able to give him all of her milk and more
than he could eat of other food. In fact, various kinds of
bones were lying around the mouth of the den gathering
flies.

One evening Coyote went far down in the burrow to
look it over. She saw fallen earth and stones clogging up
parts of it. At once she started to dig, the pup nosing
along behind her. When she backed out, he went far
in ahead of her and began to look for possible food. The
mother went back in to dig hard at a rock that stood in
the way. The pup had managed somehow to squeeze
past it to reach the round chamber at the end of the
tunnel.

A rumbling and thudding noise caused the mother to
stop work. It continued for several seconds. Coyote nosed
about in the dark and found the passage ahead filled completely with earth and fallen stones. The roof of rocks
had fallen in. She whined several times to the pup, then
barked, the short commanding bark that pups always
heeded. Then she crawled outside and barked, ending

with a long-drawn-out howl. There was no response. Down the burrow she went, digging, pulling at the stones with her teeth. Everything was so tightly jammed that she could make no headway. All that night and into the morning she dug and dug and tore with her teeth, then she would back out and howl.

When the nurse and the little girl arrived as usual they found the coyote stretched out on the new heap of earth at the burrow's entrance. They thought she was dead, but when they came close, Coyote rose to her feet unsteadily and moved among the rock piles until she could slip away in the direction of the woods. The nurse examined the burrow and saw that there had been a big cave-in. She told the child that the little coyote must be dead. The little girl would not eat anything that afternoon. All the food they brought was left for the mother wolf.

When nurse and child reached the Horton home at four-thirty and told the story to Mrs. Horton, she tried to reach her husband at his office. He and the two boys, who were in town that day, had gone to the movies. By the time they returned it was growing dark, but at once they hunted up flashlights and shovels and all three started on the run for the ruins.

They went straight to the burrow and soon saw that it would be hopeless to dig. A whole wall of stones had sunk part way into the earth at the place where the burrow should have been. Mr. Horton started to toss rocks out of the way but soon gave it up.

"Anyway," he said to the boys, "the young coyote can't be anything but dead. When that wall collapsed, the little fellow no doubt died instantly. I'm glad that our old friend, the mother, wasn't in the burrow too. She seems to have a charmed life."

While they were trudging home through the dew-soaked grass, Mr. Horton talked further. "I think our coyote," he said, "is quite a character. I believe she learned to like us just as a dog would. She keeps well away from strangers, as you know. And it looks as if she and your little sister are especially close friends, probably because animals trust and tolerate the young. I'm glad to see this friendship."

Before they reached the house they heard a single howl, a long, sad wail. Mr. Horton looked back, then he turned to the boys.

"That's mother love for you," he said. "She won't forget that pup, the last one of all those she's tried to raise in these two years. Now she's alone. I wonder what she'll do. She might come back to stay with us. Yes, I wonder!"

When the little girl and her nurse went to the ruins next day, Coyote rose from her lookout post and stood regarding them. The child ran forward to within a few feet and talked to her, the nurse made no objection, according to her instructions. Next the little girl threw pieces of sandwich to Coyote, who picked them up one at a time and returned to her post to eat. She was wary, but certainly not afraid. Presently she trotted away.

Before the child had started back to the house, the wolf returned carrying a dead young rabbit in her mouth. This she laid at the entrance of the burrow, where two other small rabbits were already lying. She whined, as if calling her young one to come and eat. Then she dug a little at the choked burrow as if believing that the young one must sometime come out. The little girl watched her and wanted to help.

On the following day the child brought a toy shovel and dug hard at the burrow. She felt very sorry for the dead rabbits lying there and later buried them nearby while Coyote watched. The same thing happened on the two following days. Coyote continued to bring little rabbits for her young one, and the child always buried them.

There came a day when there were no rabbits at the burrow's entrance, but on that afternoon the wolf brought a young woodchuck, which she laid in front of the child. The child scolded her this time in her childish way, but Coyote did not understand, trotted away, and came back with a dead meadow mouse. She seemed perfectly satisfied when the little girl buried these offerings, believing, as Mr. Horton pointed out, that the child was putting them away as caches to be eaten at a future time.

"I wonder," said Mr. Horton, "if Coyote hasn't now somehow confused our daughter with her own young one, or else adopted her. Mother love even in a wolf seems to be so strong that it must be lavished on someone."

"I'm worried about all this!" complained Mrs. Horton.

"You needn't be," her husband assured her. "It all seems safe to me, but it's very remarkable. It's an experience our child should never forget. She's getting to be more and more fond of that animal."

The hot days of late June brought little change except that the nurse and the child now sat in the shade of a tall maple tree behind the ruins. At once Coyote, too, changed her position and took her stand on a mound nearby. The wolf brought no more dead animals to the child, but always shared in the afternoon snack of sandwich, cookies, and sometimes cake, which she now took carefully from the little girl's hand. The child patted her nose and Coyote cavorted around her, wagging her tail in a great show of happiness. The nurse had no part in this. Everything was between the child and the wolf.

"I want to take the children to the seashore," Mrs. Horton declared every day or two.

"Wait," counseled her husband. "The boys are all right here and I just can't see our daughter separated from the coyote. It might hurt both of them very much."

"You like that wolf," complained Mrs. Horton. "I don't. After all, it's just a wild animal."

"Yes, but it's showing human traits. It seems to have adopted our daughter. It has had an opportunity to show it's more than just an ordinary wild animal, and it has become a friend. Don't spoil this!"

Mrs. Horton sniffed but said nothing more. She felt sure that sooner or later she would gain her point.

Coyote was once more contented. She liked the old ruins, the plentiful wild animals, the pleasantly warm days and especially the association with the child. Never before had she been so relaxed. At evening she sat on the lookout slab and watched the day birds go to bed in hiding places such as the dense foliage. Then she saw the little brown bats fly forth from holes in the old walls and catch insects on the wing, and the deer in their red summer coats troop slowly from the woods. Even the big buck left the thickets early in the evening at this time of year. Rabbits would be hopping from the woods to eat clover, and the old black and white skunk would be coming from the ruins leading her solemn brood of eight little black and whites. Except for the hum and chirp of insects, all would be very still until the big horned owls hooted. Coyote herself was very quiet these nights. There was no other wolf to whom she could call or with whom she could sing.

Chapter 12

THE FOXES, both the red and the gray, had for some time abandoned the park area but were still numerous in nearby counties. Suddenly, among them appeared the terrible disease hydrophobia, or rabies. It drove those who contracted it mad, and, before they died, made them want to bite not only other foxes but all animals they encountered. The contagious disease was spread through their saliva.

Dogs were not immune unless inoculated against it, and if a human were bitten by a rabid creature a long and painful treatment with a special serum was necessary to save life. No one could find out how the disease started or how to stamp it out except by inoculating all dogs and killing the foxes. They were the animals that could most easily bite.

Mr. Horton explained all of this to his family and had his three terriers freshly inoculated and penned up. He was sure that they would want to run to any fox or strange dog they saw, and that then they would certainly be bitten. The rabid animals had a tendency in their madness to travel for many miles around the country until they fell from exhaustion; so the disease could not be restricted to one area.

The newspapers and the radio continually harped on the danger and warned that all dogs in particular should be watched, for unfortunately a pet dog, if he went mad, was just as bad as a strange one.

"Keep away from all strange dogs until this thing is over," Mr. Horton advised. "And watch the wolf, Nurse. If she does anything peculiar, out of the ordinary, while you are near her, bring our daughter home at once. Until there is some definite word of rabies right here in this community, I see no reason to keep anyone indoors."

Never were the days more beautiful than during July. The nurse regularly took her charge out to the ruins, where the child loved to play. They stayed until the air cooled and the dew began to form on the grass in low places. Coyote was always there to greet them and playfully romp around the child. Sometimes she stayed all afternoon; at other times she vanished in the woods before they left.

One day, while Coyote lolled on her favorite lookout mound, there were the sounds of distant automobile horns and several gunshots. Up jumped Coyote, ready to run for the woods. The nurse looked up from her book, then resumed reading. She was not imaginative and felt little curiosity. The fact that birds were rising from the field next to the ruins and flying away as if disturbed did not register with her.

A scream from the child changed all this. The nurse saw the little girl running desperately toward her, chased by a big black and white hairy dog with an open mouth.

The child, screaming, stumbled, and fell with the dog leaping on top of her. The brave nurse rushed toward them without any weapon, but the coyote shot past her and threw herself on the dog.

"The two rolled over together with fearful noises," the nurse told reporters after she had come back from the hospital, where she was inoculated. "The dog pulled free and ran for me, leaping up in the air to get me by the elbow. That really hurt, too. I struck at him with the other hand and he turned away but not because I hit him so hard. I believe he had no sense of feeling. He ran back to the child and again had the wolf at his throat. The wolf looked very small but she certainly had pluck. She hung on and pulled this way and that until the dog rose on his hind legs and hurled her to one side.

"It was awful. The noise! The fighting! The dust! The dog came for me again and I tripped and fell over a rock, but the wolf followed him and seized his hind leg. The dog, dragging the wolf, couldn't reach me, so he turned and bit at the wolf. The two didn't seem to separate again. They just rolled. Just as I was getting up I heard a tremendous bang and saw two men with guns right in front of me. They shot twice at the dog, then they helped me to my feet and got the crying child from where she'd crawled among the rock piles.

"I took a look at that big black dog lying there. His mouth was open and I never saw such teeth. The whole front of him was soaked with water or saliva and his legs were all caked with mud. Beside him lay the wolf, that wonderful wolf who saved me and the child. She, too, was dead. I felt so sorry. I said to the men, 'This wolf saved our lives!'

" 'What!' they cried, as if they couldn't believe it. 'The wolf!'

" 'Yes, that wolf,' I told them. 'She fought the dog.'

"I found then that my white clothes were all red from the tear in my hurt arm, but I worried only for the child. Believe it or not, she hadn't a scratch! The dog must have bitten only her dress before the wolf struck him.

"About twenty men were around us then. They came fast across the field in automobiles. Most of them carried guns.

"One of them said to me, 'We've been following that rabid dog all over town.'

" 'Rabid!' said I. 'Why, we'll all go mad!' But they said they'd take me straight to the hospital for treatment and it would be all right. Then they got to talking about the wolf.

" 'It's an awful shame not to do something about her,' said one man. They admired her slim body, and her brown-gray color, and declared that she looked like a little thoroughbred race horse.

"One of them said, 'I'll put her in my car and bury her properly at home with a headstone.'

"But then up came Mr. and Mrs. Horton all out of breath. They sure were worried. They hugged their child and then they even hugged me. I told them it was the wolf that saved us. Then Mr. Horton began examining the wolf and said in that big voice of his, 'I believe she's not dead.' That certainly surprised everyone.

"Well, Mrs. Horton and I took turns carrying the child to the house and Mr. Horton carried the wolf. He phoned a vet doctor when we got there and the vet gave the wolf an inoculation against rabies first of all, then got to work on bringing it around. She was cut up considerable around the neck and shoulders and bleeding bad, but what seemed to have knocked her unconscious was a couple of pellets of shot that plowed along her skull.

"The wolf was laid in our nice pen and all bedded down in straw. People came from all over to see her. Mr. Horton made the vet stay right there till she came to and could move around. She was a little shaky on her feet but getting to look better all the time. There were a dozen or more people at the pen and they really cheered then. Everybody was happy, but most of all I was. I can't help praising that wolf!"

This was the nurse's story. Much impressed, the reporters took numerous photographs and wrote detailed accounts of the remarkable happenings.

As an aftermath there came offers for the coyote from two important zoos and a traveling circus, but Mr. Horton would not think of giving her up.

"You can see she's like one of my family," he explained. "You can have any of our other pets but not her. No, I want to give her a home as long as she lives. This isn't a case of just any old wolf!"

Coyote knew exactly where she was. Here was her old pen, the floor concrete now and the wire new and heavier. And she was not afraid of any of the Hortons. Mr. Horton went into her pen and fed her with his own hands. He brought the little girl in sometimes so that the friendship between these two would not ever lessen. And again he placed a collar around Coyote's neck and gradually induced her to accept being led with a cord. After that he and his boys tried to be on hand every evening to take her for a walk in the fields. He doubted whether she would run away, but because the local game warden worried over the possibility of her again starting a pack, he agreed to precautions.

Now, after her experiences in the woods, Coyote knew how to treat the three terriers. They were still hostile but tried to rush her only once. At this time she was being led on a long leash. The terriers saw her and came on the run, all three yapping. As each one came within range of her spring, he was hurled to one side. She was so quick that the dog did not quite know what hit him. One of them came back for more and got it. This time she threw him on his back and menaced his throat. Suddenly the terriers got the idea that they had better keep out of her way. Mr. Horton and his boys were watching and could see that Coyote actually was trying not to hurt the dogs.

On their walks together, sometimes alone, sometimes with the two boys or their sister, Coyote showed Mr. Horton many new things. She never passed the grass nest of a meadow mouse without digging it up, or a rabbit in its well-hidden bed without trying to leap upon it. She could scent a mole or a shrew in its underground tunnel and unearth it with lightning speed. Chipmunks she stalked with unerring skill. And she seemed to know wherever there were late raspberries, wineberries, and blackberries.

Coyote caught green frogs and pounced on harmless snakes along the streams. The spotted leopard frogs seemed to be too smelly to lure her, and she rarely bothered with toads, as if she knew that unpleasant acid could be exuded from their skins. Her nose was always at work, sifting the various scents constantly encountered. And so Mr. Horton was learning much about denizens of his own fields and woods.

Visitors came nearly every day to see Coyote. They frightened her and caused her to retreat to her barrel in the rear of the pen. One day when Jeremy came, she smelled him from afar and hid herself. He left without seeing more than her nose.

Coyote was never contented in confinement. She showed that she hated it. She spent most of every night trotting around and around the pen, sometimes scratching at the corners to find a way out, sometimes trying to climb the wire. She howled occasionally at night, always the lonesome call, never the happy song of the woodlands.

"I don't know what to do with her," Mr. Horton exclaimed one evening when listening to her sad howl. "I guess, after all, she's just a wild thing and can't be fully tamed. She's had her freedom and she craves to get back to the woods. I guess I'd feel the same way in a pen."

The one contentment in Coyote's life seemed to come from her affection for the little girl. The child fascinated her and she fascinated the child. When they were together, they were like devoted playmates. Coyote was forever licking the child's hands, fussing over her, trying to play with her. The little girl could roll her around, pull her ears, examine her teeth, in fact do anything she wanted. It changed Coyote when the child was taken to the seashore for two weeks.

The wolf came to the wire and looked expectantly whenever she heard anyone approaching. When she saw it was not the child, she turned away forlornly. This went on day after day. Mr. Horton watched it with misgivings.

After ten days of loneliness, Coyote made up her mind; she was going to get out of her pen and go back to the ruins. That night she worked methodically at the wire with her teeth until she broke a strand. Once a hole was started the rest was easier. She managed to get her back teeth to work, the ones she used to shear meat and crack bones. Twisting and pulling, she made the hole a little bigger. Presently she could force her head through. When the hole was scarcely large enough to let in a cat, she forced through one shoulder as well as her head. Slowly, painfully, the remainder of her body followed. She stood outside, free.

Chapter 13

COYOTE loped to the ruins. They were gloomy indeed, for the sky was overcast and the light of the stars could scarcely filter through. Her eyes were keen enough, however, to guide her, and her nose was hard at work. She circled the place carefully, sniffing in every corner but finding nothing of interest to her. There was no trace of her offspring, no trace of her friend the little girl. She mounted her favorite observation post and howled the lonesome call.

In a light rain that came before dawn she loped to the parks and made her way almost to the Delaware River. It was country well known to her, and well liked in the days past. Now it was dreary and frightening. She missed companionship more than ever before.

In the light of day, three white-tailed deer watched her approach and scarcely went out of her way. They could see that she was not on a hunt. A gray squirrel barked at her from a low limb, and her old enemies, the crows, on their way from their roost to the farm land, swung low to caw derisively before continuing their journey. This was the time of day when she should be hiding in some safe thicket, but, instead, she felt like looking over more of her old haunts.

She trotted from place to place. Here was the burrow where she had caught an especially wary woodchuck and later a rabbit, there a patch of thick grass always harboring mice, and over to the right another woodchuck burrow and a path to the woods used by opossums and skunks. On and on she went. In the farm land men were working in the cornfields, cutting and gathering with harvesting machines to fill their silos for cattle feed. In an alfalfa patch a final crop was being mowed. The sounds were the same as always: the continuous hum of autos, an occasional horn, the toot of the electric trains, the drone of distant airplanes and whistles from factories. From the direction of the park, where the Boy Scouts had a camp, someone was blowing a bugle.

Coyote turned toward the Pennypack Creek above where it entered the boundary of the park. The water was low from lack of heavy rain, and she could easily cross at many places. Schools of minnows loafed in the quiet shallows near shore, away from the larger fish that would eat them. Frogs crouched in the grass and a brownish-black snake was coiled on a piece of driftwood. Tracks in the bare mud still bore the scent of raccoons, muskrats, and weasels that had traveled at night. Higher on the bank, among the trees, were runways of rabbits and signs of places where gray squirrels had buried cones laden with seed. This was still the time of plenty before frosts and autumn storms had changed the foliage and gunners and trappers had killed many of the wild things.

Examining the creek's bank, Coyote found where both raccoons and muskrats had lugged fresh-water clams

from their water beds and had cleverly unhinged their double shells to expose the tender meat. There were tracks of barn rats that used the edge of the creek as a road to take them from one house to another. On a log in a quiet pool, two turtles were sunning, heads up and ready to push themselves into the water at the first sign of danger, while two watchful sandpipers rested undisturbed on a mud island close by.

Coyote crossed the creek at a shallow riffle, taking care to step where deer had gone across and shown the place to be safe. While in the stream, she saw two fishermen not far up the creek, and made haste to reach cover. An old path took her up the hill to the edge of a hayfield, where she had to dodge into the bushes to escape a swarm of angry yellow jackets that rose from a hole in the ground under her. She sighted a fat brown woodchuck running for his burrow, and she had him at bay with a few long jumps. Then came the usual springing in and away until she could seize him by the neck. Too much for one meal, a part of him was buried in a shady spot. She found a nearby wild apple tree with ripe apples on the ground. Two of these she ate; then she stopped beside a field where she could see a long distance over the grass. Resting in the shade of bushes, she curled up and tried to sleep.

In the afternoon, at the time when the nurse and the little girl usually came to the ruins, Coyote recrossed the creek and anxiously hurried through the woods. At once she saw that something was wrong. A cloud of blue smoke hung over the place. Circling warily, she saw two men burning great heaps of brush they had cut from around the old walls. Gone was all the attraction of the place as well as its safety. Sadly, the wolf turned away. Another wonderful thing in her life was gone.

Coyote trotted to the border of the park, not knowing what to do next, but she encountered picnickers there at every turn. She listened to them shouting and laughing, then, low in spirits, slunk away. Things were not as they used to be.

She sang her song that evening, alone on a small wooded hill. "Yap, yap, yap woooooo," repeated several times. Only distant dogs answered, barking angrily. Crestfallen, she retreated into the thicker woods. The world was against her. After that, she trotted into the farm country: the worst thing she could have done. Her enemy the police dog, with three small hounds as hunting companions, was on the prowl that night.

The owner of the hounds had deliberately let them loose by themselves to get into good shape to hunt for him when the gunning season opened. They were perfectly happy without the police dog, but he had joined them for the hunt and could not be left behind. They bayed on the trail of rabbits and had a wonderful time until they came upon the tracks of the coyote. This was something different!

Silently the hounds followed the tracks. They would have left the trail had not the police dog shown excitement and encouraged them to continue to follow it. Gradually the hounds warmed up to this new scent. They knew nothing about wolves, but they enjoyed using their keen noses to work out an intricate tangle of tracks. Soon they were moving fast, following Coyote and baying happily, the police dog tagging after them.

Coyote listened and soon realized that they were following her. She ran to the creek and tried to break the scent trail, but the smart police dog led the hounds across. They followed her no matter where she ran. For nearly an hour she circled around the woods without being able to throw them off the track, though they could not get close to her. If only she had had her first litter to help her, ready to fight and strong enough to hold their own against most dogs! She knew that she had to keep on running, somehow stay ahead of the pursuers that could not be shaken off the trail.

At close to eleven o'clock she was still running, tired now, and very worried. In desperation she went to the houses beyond the farm country, dodging among the bushes on the lawns. At one point she was at the house where Caesar, the Airedale, lived. If only he would help her! She called wildly. There was no answer. She turned away.

Suddenly there was an animal running almost beside her in the moonlight. Caesar had heard and had come. She turned to him and he saw the desperate state she was in. The two stood side by side as the hounds came scurrying through the bushes. They were met by the wolf and the dog. Two against three, but the three hounds were cowards and, after looking in surprise, actually began to retreat. It was then that the police dog caught up. He sized up the situation in a moment and threw himself at the little wolf. She tried to dodge but went down under his weight, fighting frantically.

Caesar went for the police dog. The dog was busy with the wolf and Caesar had a chance to seize him by the side of the head. He found the hide tough, but he chewed with all his might. The two rolled over. Caesar lost his hold and the police dog seized him by the back of the neck and actually shook him. Caesar chewed the nearest leg and the other dog had to roll over to throw him off. Now they leaped at each other and rolled again, teeth clashing. Caesar knew that he was outclassed, but he was game. It never occurred to him to run.

Meanwhile the three hounds came back and surrounded Coyote. They growled and bayed evilly and made furious passes at her, but were afraid to come to grips. Backed up against a bush, with teeth bared, she faced them and made a wicked leap every time a hound came close. When she struck an ear or a nose or even a shoulder, she bit and ripped.

Suddenly the police dog had Caesar really down and was boring into his neck. Only his collar saved him. As it was, he was choked almost to death. Losing interest in the Airedale when he seemed no longer a menace, the police dog turned to go for the wolf.

Coyote saw him coming and dashed past the hounds. Across the lawn she ran with them in full cry behind her and the police dog bringing up the rear. She headed across two other lawns separated by low wire fences that she leaped and the dogs had to climb. Now she had a good lead and made the most of it.

When they were closing in on her again she put on a wild burst of speed and headed for her old house, Mr. Horton's. Just what to do then she had not thought out. Thudding behind her came the police dog, more eager than the hounds.

They were almost neck and neck when they dashed among the animal pens, around them over to the Horton house, around it and back to the pens. The hounds were making a great noise with their excited baying, chickens whose coops were upset squawked, ducks quacked, then there was a different kind of music, for two beehives belonging to the boys had been turned over and the furious bees had found a chance to take revenge on the hounds before they got past. Yelps and yowls came from all three as they scattered.

A shaft of light appeared from an open door, and to this went the desperate Coyote. She flashed in just ahead of the police dog, who followed so fast he hit Mr. Horton's legs.

Coyote found herself in a hallway with stairs at the far end. She had never before seen stairs, but up them she went with the dog crowding her from behind. Now she went along another hall and ran into a room that had an open door. The dog was so close that she could not look around; she could only run behind or over furniture, right across the low bed and through the door again. A scream or two from the bed's startled occupant made no difference to either Coyote or the dog. They entered another room, dashed over the bed, and scared the occupant, then down the stairs they scrambled and rolled.

Mr. Horton was ready and waiting. He held a tennis racket and stood in the middle of the hallway in the full glare of the lights. He let Coyote dash past him, but turned the dog aside with a powerful swing of the racket. He did not hurt the dog, he simply deflected him from his course. Coyote dodged into a room at the right of the front door and was out of sight.

Mr. Horton quickly shifted his position to the entrance of this room and held off the dog with the racket. There was a dangerous moment when the dog faced him with bared teeth, but even the terrific excitement of the chase could not completely change the dog's instinctive servility in relation to man. He slunk away. Quickly Mr. Horton opened the front door and ushered him out. Then he walked to the room where Coyote had taken refuge.

Chapter 14

Coyote had hidden behind a sofa. When Mr. Horton walked around the room and found her there, she was crouching in a corner, her head low, almost even with the floor, but her eyes looked up at him with an expression he had never before seen. It was a hopeless, wistful look as if the wolf were trying to say, "There's nothing left in this world for me, but how I wish it were different." Coyote just stayed like that, her sides heaving and her eyes telling a story.

Mr. Horton was touched. He spoke to her in a kindly voice, trying to reassure her, but she did not move. The household was downstairs now, in various odd night costumes, all of them frightened and wanting to find out what had happened.

"I don't quite know," was Mr. Horton's answer. "I heard the same racket you did, barking, crashing, howling, and as I had not yet gone to bed, I opened the front door and looked out. Then in a flash in rushed Coyote with a huge black and brown police dog at her heels. They took no notice of me. They just dashed upstairs and down, and then I managed somehow to make the dog go out of the house. Coyote hid here in the library, just about all in. She's behind the sofa and won't move. Take a look but don't frighten her. She's the saddest-looking animal you'll ever see."

One after another, they peered over the back of the sofa, then edged away. The nurse was holding the little girl in her arms so that she too could see Coyote. The child had been frightened by all the noise, and when now she looked at her playmate crouching there so forlorn and desperate, she suddenly began to sob. The nurse let her slide down to the floor, and the little girl broke from her and ran to the sofa. Before any of the startled family could stop her, she had thrown herself down beside the wolf and was stroking her rumpled coat. Mrs. Horton gasped and sprang forward in alarm, but her husband restrained her.

Presently the little girl came from behind the sofa, and with her the wolf, who was licking her right hand and rubbing a shoulder against the child. The girl sat down on the floor and the wolf crouched beside her, licking now her right cheek as seriously as if her life depended upon it. And who can say that it did not depend upon it?

"I can't stand any more of this!" cried out Mrs. Horton. "I'm going to pick up Helen and take her straight to bed."

"No, no," warned her husband. "Coyote in her nervous state might resent it. Better call the child to you, then take her away. And everybody, don't let the terriers out of the kitchen! We've had enough doings here for one night." He thought to himself, "How fortunate that Helen came home from the seashore today!"

How much one little wolf could disrupt family life

was shown in the morning. When the maid came from her own home to do the cooking for the Hortons, she expected the terriers to run outside, but she had to drive them out. They wanted to get through the kitchen door to the dining room. Finally she let them come in again and go to the dining room. But they did not stop there. They ran into the hall, then into the library, where pandemonium started at once and in a big way.

In their own home the terriers felt that they had rights and they flew at Coyote as an interloper. She tried to avoid a fight, ran all around the room, even over the chairs, then into the hall. Here the terriers caught up with her and fastened themselves to her flanks like biting leeches. She had to fight and she did. All over the hall, the four rolled amid yipping, yapping, and shrieking. Coyote did not bite as much as she slashed. It was not her idea to kill; as usual she just wanted to defend herself. Against one at a time, or even two, it might have been easy, but three at once were a real difficulty to her now.

Mr. Horton and the two boys dashed downstairs, though only half dressed.

"Quick! Help me throw this rug over them!" Mr. Horton cried.

They lifted the rug and tossed it over the seething mass of howling, yapping animals. At once the dogs began breaking from under it, frightened by the darkness and the enveloping weight. All three were bloody and still wildly excited.

"Out!" shouted Mr. Horton. One of the boys held the front door open while the other boy and his father chased out the dogs one by one. Coyote pulled herself last from under the rug and slunk straight to her corner behind the sofa. She did not limp or seem to be hurt, but she looked miserable.

"Oh, my!" exclaimed Mr. Horton. "What can be coming next! Look at the floor! Blood, hair, dirt! Look at you and me, all hot and dusty. My! I've had enough of it for a while! Let's dress, get breakfast and then tackle this problem again."

Seated around the table, the family could talk of nothing but the coyote. Didn't they owe her a lot for her defense of Helen from the mad dog? Wasn't she their problem anyway because they were the cause of her being brought to the East?

"I don't care!" exclaimed Mr. Horton. "She's going to a zoo as fast as we can get her there. It's plain to see we can't keep her penned up, for she escapes. She can't be made a pet around the house because she's an unpredictable wolf, not just a tabby cat. If she is turned out in the woods, she raises a pack every year, and since wolves must live largely on meat, they kill. The Police Department will get after me, not to mention my sportsmen friends. So far I've been very lucky. No bills for chickens, geese, ducks, fallow deer, goats, sheep, and chewed-up dogs. I tell you, the zoo is the place for a wolf." Then he added, "But how I hate to send *her* there!" As if to make matters worse, at that moment Coyote limped into the breakfast room, wagging her tail, then trying to prance ingratiatingly.

"I give up!" Mr. Horton said, almost sadly. "I know I can't send our wolf to a zoo."

"Hurray!" shouted both of his boys. They went to the hall closet to get Coyote's lead strap with her collar attached. When they approached her, she lay on the floor and rolled over on her back in surrender. "We'll take her for a walk and give her water and a good breakfast," they said. "She's not much hurt!"

"Don't let the terriers get at her," warned their father, but they laughed at this.

"If they went for her out in the open where she considers she has as much right as they have, she'd eat them up!" replied Tom, his elder son. "She's like that. We all know about her from the times when we walked her before. She's terrific! The terriers know about that, too."

The telephone rang and Mr. Horton went to answer it.

"Oh, this is Bill Thorpe, is it? How do, Bill. What's that? You ask whether the wolf came my way last night? I don't understand. What's on your mind? Oh, you say that every time she comes around something happens to your dog, Caesar. What's happened to him now? You say he got very badly bitten last night in a big fight? Do you think he is going to be all right? Good! Well, don't worry any more about the wolf. She's going out of circulation. Yes, that's it. I agree with you entirely. This isn't the Wild West. Good-by, Bill, and pat that fine, good old Caesar for me, and for the wolf!" Then Mr. Horton really chuckled.

"I've found out something I often suspected. Caesar must be Coyote's boy friend! Well, I might know she'd pick something pretty good. He's a thoroughbred. But what a joke on quiet old Bill Thorpe!"

Mr. Horton was late in reaching his office that day. In fact, he spent all morning reinforcing Coyote's pen and testing its concrete floor. When he was satisfied that it would hold her he led Coyote into it and took off her collar. He expected her to try to get out, but she went meekly into her barrel and lay down.

When Mr. Horton reached his office, he put in a person-to-person call to Uncle Harry. These two had a talk that was long, considering the distance.

"Yes, the coyote's just fine," Mr. Horton said after his greeting, "but we can't keep her around here any more. She's too much wolf when she gets loose, and she raises too many young wolves. That's right; she's a real pet with us and all of us are mighty fond of her, but we're licked. Now, I phoned to find out if you could let her loose in the Arizona desert where you found her. I'll ship her by plane to Tucson in a safe crate. We want her to be all right for the rest of her life, and what's better than putting her out where coyotes really belong? Isn't that lots better for her than being penned up in a zoo? You agree? Oh, I'm glad to hear that. And you'll arrange things? Fine! I'll send her to you in two days."

Then Mr. Horton sighed rather sadly, for Coyote had made life on the farm exciting and she had certainly been an affectionate pet for the family whenever she was with them.

Now that he had made up his mind about the wolf, Mr. Horton went ahead quickly with all the details. He himself shoved her gently into the crate in spite of her desperate objections. He even saw her safely placed aboard the plane. The boys were at school and missed most of this, but little Helen was allowed to say good-by before the crate was placed in the truck at the farm. The wolf licked her hand through the wired door, and never took her eyes from the child while she was in view.

"The saddest thing I ever saw!" whispered the good nurse.

Chapter 15

UNCLE HARRY could be called a devoted Westerner. He liked the wild desert and the even wilder mountains, and he liked them largely because of the many creatures he found there. Sometimes he amused himself by wondering how he would manage to live if he were a wolf or a mountain lion, an antelope or something else instead of a human being. In the end, he always decided that if he were given a choice he would rather be a coyote. In that case, he argued, he would not be restricted to one type of food or one type of locality. Indeed, he could eat almost anything and live almost anywhere; be big enough to hold his own, yet small enough to hide. And what eyes, ears, and nose he would have!

"But," he said to himself, "something seemed to be wrong with the idea of a coyote living now in the East. And I'm glad that the one I gave to the Horton boys is coming back where she belongs."

Uncle Harry's Arizona ranch was well outside of town in what was called foothill country. Not far away the mountains rose steeply, largely bare of vegetation but harboring small creatures and even a few of the rare mountain sheep. The ranch kept two horses and a small flock of goats, but, above all, it maintained a well that supplied water to endless numbers of creatures that otherwise would scarcely be able to exist there. Uncle Harry saw to it that water was pumped daily into a huge open trough that overflowed into a natural pool. Here many birds, small animals, and even the timid antelope came hurriedly to gulp down several mouthfuls of precious fluid, then hasten back to the bushes where they felt safe.

This was desert country with little rain. Animals and insects survived by getting necessary moisture to tide them over the long period of drought from the kinds of desert plants that stored water in their roots, stems, and leaves. These plants were of great importance. The birds and small animals that ate insects often did not need more moisture than they found in the bodies of their prey, the insects having, for the most part, secured moisture from plants. It was much the same with the meat eaters, who found juices in the flesh they consumed. In one way or another, the desert areas managed to support a great number and variety of wild creatures, but generally these were very thirsty except in the rainy season, and there were times when, without Uncle Harry's well, many would have suffered and perhaps died on the ranch.

No one realized this better than kindly Uncle Harry. He knew, too, that coyotes, who had to be energetic, required more water than many other kinds of animals. Nearly every day he could see coyotes, ones that stayed on or near the ranch within easy reach of the water. Coyotes all looked alike to some people, but to him each one had its own special character. There were nine there at the time when Coyote was delivered to the airport and brought out to the ranch. Five of these were young ones born that spring and not quite full grown. These belonged to the pair that stayed nearest to the mountains, the other old pair preferred the flat country toward the south and rarely came to the water.

Uncle Harry was pretty sure that Coyote would identify herself with the nearest, the family of seven. Certainly she would not want to live alone in the desert. But how to introduce her was the important question, for Uncle Harry knew that jealousy against a newcomer could result in serious trouble in the animal world.

Uncle Harry, like Mr. Horton, had a dog yard with concrete floor and wire on sides and top. Coyote was brought to this. Uncle Harry quietly opened the crate and waited for the coyote to rush out, but she crouched in the farthest corner and would not move. The two hired men wanted to poke or shake her out, but Uncle Harry would have none of that and made them move away. He talked to her in a low voice while slowly walking around the pen so she could see that he meant no harm. Finally he sat down on the box in the pen that was her sleeping quarters.

Twenty minutes later he was still sitting on the box and Coyote had not moved, but presently she appeared at the entrance of her crate, looking out and all around her. There was no sign of fear now, just curiosity. She stepped out and walked around the edge of the pen until she came within three paces of Uncle Harry. Here she stopped and stood looking at him for nearly a minute with the intelligent expression characteristic of her.

He avoided gazing straight into her yellowish eyes and

tried to show no particular interest. If he made a good start with her, he was fairly sure that she would be friendly and no more afraid of him than of the Hortons. He hoped that she would turn into a wonderful pet for him and his wife while at the same time living a free life.

He ate his dinner sitting on the box in Coyote's pen, and he took care to toss tidbits in front of her from time to time. A few of these she ate, others she carried around in her mouth and dropped at one end of the pen. Evidently she was trying to find a place in which to bury them until she was hungry. By this time she had licked and shaken her furry coat into perfect shape and was a beautiful, sleek, brown and gray animal, more trim and spry-looking than any dog.

After two days Uncle Harry could touch Coyote. Then she seemed to have lost all fear of him and of his wife, though remaining very suspicious of all others. He carefully fitted a chain collar around her neck, one that other coyotes could not chew to pieces, and now before the evening feeding time he opened the gate and pushed her out. The goats, he knew, were safely penned.

She showed great excitement when she was free. At once she started to run into the desert, while Uncle Harry's spirits sank and he feared that he had lost her. But that was Coyote's way of celebrating her release. After a few minutes she came running back, entered her pen, and drank from her bucket. Then she squirmed and pranced around the surprised man and wagged her tail like any happy dog. Uncle Harry was very pleased. Her dish of scraps and dog meal was ready for her and, for the first time since her arrival, she ate with enthusiasm, not seeming to care when the gate of her pen was closed.

Next day the goats and the horses were led in front of her pen, one by one. The goats she watched very carefully, but she took little interest in the horses.

"She'll kill the goats," said Uncle Harry to his wife. "That is to say she'll kill them unless we convince her she must not do it."

"I hope not," answered his wife, who liked all of them and often fed them.

That evening, Uncle Harry fastened a lead cord to her collar and led her to the goats that were feeding among the low bushes behind the ranch house. When Coyote first saw them she crouched and froze to the spot. Several were brown in color and looked like deer. Uncle Harry led her around and among them, scolding her when she attempted to bolt toward them. Accompanied by his wife, he did the same thing on two more occasions. After that, Coyote seemed to take little notice of the flock.

"She's intelligent; she's beginning to understand," thought the man. "But she's well fed now—will she kill one if she's hungry and gets the chance?"

The wild coyotes usually sang their song at evening and again at dawn, and once Coyote sang with them from her pen. The wild ones stopped at once. They were some distance away at the foot of a hill, but they recognized a foreign voice and were upset by the knowledge that another of their kind was in the area. Guardedly they approached to investigate and did not leave until fairly well satisfied that Coyote could do them no harm. They knew, too, from her scent on the evening breeze that it was a she who had invaded their territory. This irritated the old wild female.

Uncle Harry took a chance and let Coyote have a run

in the afternoons before he fed her, and all went well until the fourth day, when she did not return. In vain both he and his wife whistled and called. At length they gave up trying to get her back that evening, but left the gate open and her food in the pen.

Coyote had run into trouble. She had gone farther out on the plain than usual and had been waylaid by the band of seven coyotes. She was surrounded before she realized what was happening, and she had had no previous experience of this kind. Coyotes were approaching from all sides through the low creosote bushes, none of them quite hostile as yet but all ready to take advantage of any wrong move on her part. On the air was their scent, the strong scent of the plains wolf.

Coyote stood looking from one to the other for several seconds. All of them appeared grim. As a pack they were formidable and she was an alien, all alone in a land strange to her. Dogs she might have outrun, but she had no way of knowing how fast these animals of her own kind could go. She was frightened but knew that she must not show fear.

Slowly the pack closed in and still she stood motionless. Now they were almost upon her, studying her and sniffing, the young ones following the example of their parents and waiting to be shown what to do. The father was the one to make the big decision, and he was making up his mind. He and Coyote were facing each other, very close and very wary. Then suddenly both of them relaxed. The big male coyote whined and wagged his tail like a dog. Suddenly both were prancing and sidling around and against each other like old friends.

This was too much for the mate of the big coyote to

stand for. Her jealousy came in a fit of fury and she
leaped at Coyote and bowled her over. Instantly the two
were at each other's throats, rising on hind legs, falling
and rolling together, growling and howling shrilly. But
Coyote was at a disadvantage and no match for this old
plains wolf. She went down in a wild scramble and was
pinned by the throat in a throttling grip.

All would have been over for her in a few moments
had not help come from an unexpected source. The old
male leaped in and threw his mate to one side. He stood
between them, fangs bared, mane bristling, daring either
one to resume the fight. He was leader and he was acting
as peacemaker. Both his mate and Coyote shrank back.

The young coyotes came forward cautiously, ready to
make friends. They wagged their tails and sidled about
Coyote, rubbing against her and whining happily. Their
father had accepted her for the pack and that satisfied
them. Only their mother held back, nursing her jealousy.
And Coyote disliked her in every way. It was as if a feud
were started that would simmer indefinitely, ready to
burst out at any time in open warfare. Coyote was not
afraid; in fact, now she was anxious to fight again, to
humble her enemy, to show that she could beat her and
win a place in this new territory. And she admired the
big coyote who had defended her.

Chapter 16

COYOTE was so interested in the wolves that she stayed with them the remainder of the afternoon while they lolled among the boulders waiting to hunt that night in the strong light of a nearly full moon. Led by the old female, they started out together but spread out to cover much ground. Occasionally one would stop to chase a feeding mouse or a kangaroo rat. If any little rodent could not reach his burrow, he was swallowed before the other wolves could come for a share. They kept their noses and eyes constantly at work, often looking far ahead for possible danger. Although there was a breeze, the desert plants were so stiff and thorny that they did not sway or rustle. All was silent and motionless.

Suddenly a jack rabbit jumped up, a big fellow. He bounded away, but not before two of the young coyotes saw him and started in wild pursuit. The others did not seem excited. The old male trotted to the right and his mate to the left, the remainder of their children spread out quietly, and all advanced. Coyote stayed in the rear. She did not know the plan. Presently they came upon the two chasers, who, among the scrubby bushes and cactus, had lost sight of the speedy jack. They were casting about trying to find the trail.

The line of wolves advanced, each animal sniffing for the scent. There was a sudden yap as one of the pups came upon the jack crouching beside a clump of cactus. This time the big rabbit bounded back toward the spot where he had first been found. He almost ran into Coyote. She saw him coming in his long leaps, crouched until he was very near, braced her legs, then made a great spring and nearly had him. Just in time, he dodged, but now she was almost at his heels as he went skipping over the ground in a wide circle. They both put forth all their speed and neither could gain on the other.

It was then that the younger coyotes appeared and seemed to the jack to turn up wherever he headed. Bewildered, he slowed down for a moment, and in that moment lost his life, for both Coyote and the old male were upon him. When the male was sure that the jack was dead, he let go his hold and politely allowed Coyote to walk away with her heavy quarry. But she did not go far. The old female came running up, brushed past, seized the big rabbit and tried to jerk him away from her.

Coyote was taken by surprise and lost her hold, but then, in a sudden surge of anger, ran forward and seized him again. This time she had as firm a hold as her adversary. They pulled different ways and growled furiously. They were looking jealously into each other's yellowish eyes over the form of the poor rabbit. Coyote saw hate as well as fury, and something in her responded and she was all wild wolf herself, hating the very smell of the other. The two dropped the rabbit and in an instant flew at each other.

Over they rolled, fairly screaming with fury. The old male stood, almost dumbfounded, watching and wondering at such a battle. They struggled this way and that, up on their hind legs, then locked in a clinch and falling over sideways, rolling, clawing, biting until, exhausted and hot, they half lay, half crouched for a moment to get their breath. That was when the old male seemed to wake up. Leaping between them, he stuck his wide-open jaws directly in front of theirs, all his white teeth showing and ghastly growls rumbling from his throat.

There was something terrible in his look. He distracted the attention of the two fighters from each other and made them cringe. They drew away, limping, red showing on torn ears, necks, and shoulders. Presently, well apart, each was licking whatever injured spots she could reach with her tongue, taking out the dirt, stanching the flow of the blood. But gone was the big old jack. One of the youngsters had sneaked in and dragged him away.

Presently the old female stood up and walked stiffly from the scene, her head turned sideways just enough to keep a baleful eye on Coyote. Coyote stayed crouched in the same spot for a long time. She was hurt. Toward morning she hobbled in the direction of the setting moon, gradually losing the stiffness in her injured forelegs. This being new country to her, she did not know where to find water or how to secure food, and the mice and desert rats escaped well ahead of her. Morning found her near a highway, deserted at such an early hour; she wandered along it, still hoping to find water and food of some kind.

Ahead loomed a shack. Coyote approached it guardedly. She scented something familiar, something that recalled the almost forgotten day when she had wandered through this desert and had been brought to the home of the old Indian. The shack was dark now, apparently deserted.

Coyote sat on her haunches looking at the little building. There was nothing stirring in the white light of the moon. She felt lonely and very low-spirited. Raising her nose, she howled the mournful cry of a lost wolf, the famous cry that starts low, rises in volume, then slowly drifts away into nothingness. Again and again she howled, as if carried away by her sadness.

The old Indian heard it lying on his cot beside the closed door. And, well knowing the wild creatures of the desert, he understood. It was a cry for help, but also a cry for companionship. He had always had sympathy for the much-hunted wolves who, like himself, belonged to a race that once had been supreme.

Cupping his hands around his mouth, the Indian mimicked the long song of a coyote when he serenades the moon. He did it almost perfectly. It was an answer to the cry from the desert. Like magic it thrilled the heart of the lonely lost wolf crouching wretchedly among the cacti. She thought that a friend was near. Now nothing would make her leave.

Just as the sun came above the horizon like a great red ball, the old Indian rose from his cot and went out of the house with a pan of water and a piece of bread for Coyote. She hesitated to come forward, circled guardedly, but suddenly trotted to the water, lapped it up, then bolted down the bread. The old Indian recognized her, the way she trotted and held up her head. Nearby he stood studying her, remembering the first time he saw this wolf. He brought out a second piece of bread from his meager supply. He could see that she had been in a serious fight and he suspected that it was because of the animosity of a wild coyote. But how did she happen to be back here in the desert? That puzzled him.

The old Indian had some bread and canned milk for his own breakfast, then, dressed in black trousers, a faded yellow shirt, and an old black felt hat, he shuffled on his rheumatic legs down the road toward Tucson. He was heading for the home of Uncle Harry. Cars passed him and people looked at him curiously, but none stopped to give the picturesque old man a lift. He did not expect them to stop and just kept doggedly on his slow, painful journey regardless of the growing heat. He took a short cut across the hot desert rather than enter the town, and he reached the ranch just as Uncle Harry was rising from the table after his lunch.

The Indian stood in the doorway waiting for a greeting and he got a warm one. Sitting comfortably on the porch drinking well-sweetened coffee, the Indian told about the coyote.

"You say she looks all chewed up?" Uncle Harry asked. "That means she found at least one enemy. We'd better try to bring her here quickly. Will you help me?"

The Indian agreed. Soon the two were motoring up the highway.

They found Coyote lying in the weak shadow of a creosote bush. She rose stiffly to her feet and stood watching them guardedly as they walked toward her. Recognizing Uncle Harry, she suddenly wagged her tail and sidled to him with such happiness in her greeting that he was pleased. Dropping to one knee, he examined the cuts as closely as she would let him.

"Thank goodness she's kept the flies out of her wounds!" he declared. "And they're not yet infected."

Her collar was gone, but he knotted a cord around her neck and led her toward the car. She showed little fear and was all meekness, which endeared her more than ever before to her would-be benefactor.

At the ranch she was placed in her kennel. Plenty of food scraps and water made her feel more contented, and she curled up to sleep. In the late afternoon, Uncle Harry, accompanied by his wife, Eliza, took her out on a leash. Three goats were about to be milked by one of the hired men before being penned up for the night in their shed with the others. The procedure interested Coyote. She understood perfectly now that they were not to be harmed, but she also knew only too well that they were very good meat. She watched them for as long as Uncle Harry and Eliza would let her, especially the brown one that resembled a deer. Finally Coyote was led away and shut up in her own pen, however, she could still see the alluring goats and listen to them bleat.

"If she were not intelligent," thought Uncle Harry as before, "she would manage somehow to kill the goats, but she won't touch them. They are safe."

On the following afternoon, just to test her, Eliza and Uncle Harry led Coyote to the goats, which at that time were scattered among the sparse bushes, feeding on the small leaves and twig tips. One of the tame old nannies, a white one, came forward in curiosity and actually touched noses with the wolf. Coyote's muscles trembled, but she made no move. Satisfied, Uncle Harry released her from the lead rope and walked with her a short distance into the desert, noting her intense interest not only in goats but in everything she encountered. He found her digging around a pack rat's nest in a clump of cholla cactus that was so prickly it had warded off all the rat's enemies. Coyote soon gave that up. Next she cleverly dug out the shredded bark nest of a mouse from under the roots of a mesquite bush. Coyote found only one mouse, who ran out and tried to reach another hole, but did not quite succeed in escaping.

The hot desert cooled as the sun sank behind the horizon. At once the many creatures that hid in the ground or under other shade to keep them cool began to awake and stir about. What had seemed devoid of animal life fairly swarmed with creatures, large and small. Coyote instinctively leaped aside from a small rattlesnake in the brush and gingerly watched a slow-moving, fat, pink and black lizard, a poisonous Gila monster, crawl from under a boulder, occasionally sticking out his forked black tongue. Creatures that carried poison, whether small yellow jackets, wasps, scorpions, or large reptiles, had a warning scent and a warning manner. Yet all wanted, above all things, to find food that suited their particular needs. A few were on their way to the water trough.

Uncle Harry smiled when he saw Coyote come face to face with a badger. Each feared the other but would not admit it. The badger just stood his ground, but Coyote circled warily, testing the other's ability to spring and bite. In a sort of armed truce, they separated and went their respective ways. Had Coyote followed the rugged badger, she would have seen him dig into the rat's nest under the cholla cactus, regardless of thorns, and rout out two rats that Coyote might have been able to catch. They were quick enough to escape the badger.

Soon it was time to return to the ranch. Uncle Harry wanted to be sure that Coyote was safely kenneled, and he managed to catch her and attach the lead rope. The horses had been stabled and the goats were waiting in front of their shed to be driven in and closed up tight for safety during the night. Those in the ranch houses could soon sleep, without worrying over what the wild life of the desert was up to during the dark hours.

Chapter 17

COYOTE was busying herself with the pack rats that stole scraps from her food pan. She crouched motionless at a distance from their runway as if asleep, waited until a rat came cautiously toward the pan, then sprang for him. She had caught two and they were good to eat. She tried the same with the cardinals, doves, and other desert birds but found them too quick in taking wing. The hot afternoon dragged through slowly and soon semidarkness had fallen with the moon shining overhead.

Coyote sat on her haunches looking out on the desert through the mesh wire, which allowed her a good view. Far away were the mountains where her wild brethren so often stayed safely during the day. Everything was silent. But Coyote suddenly saw a motion in the bushes in front of the goat shed. Jumping up, she stood on her hind legs for a better view, her front feet well up against the wire. She could scarcely believe her eyes when she made out the forms of two goats, the brown nanny that resembled a deer and the old white one that was friendly. They stood disconsolately in front of the closed door, locked out by the careless hired men, who had thought that all were together inside when they shut up the shed.

For some time Coyote watched the goats. She saw them lie down with their feet under them for a quick jump if needed. She heard them bleat to the other goats behind the door. After a time she transferred her attention to a fat pack rat but never forgot about the goats. She knew that they did not belong outside.

At midnight she heard gentle shuffling in the bushes. Animals were coming to the water trough. Quietly rising again as high as she could stand against the wire, she watched and waited. Dimly now she could see the backs of several creatures above the creosote bushes. They were lighter in color than goats and slightly larger. They drew nearer with many stops. Directly in front of the water they stood for a long time as if afraid to put their heads down to drink. There were eight in all, three with short black curved horns clearly showing. Then Coyote caught their scent, something new to her, for she had never seen antelope before this.

One of them put down her head to drink, the others immediately followed suit. There were crowding and changing of positions, then a sudden frightened dash back into the scrub bushes. In an instant the quick animals were gone. Coyote strained her eyes but saw nothing stir. She moved to another part of the pen for a different view but still could see no movement. Back and forth she trotted, trying to find out why these animals had run away so suddenly. Then she noticed that the two goats were on their feet gazing into the desert.

Two short yaps told the story; they were the call of a coyote to bring others into a chase. Coyote understood, and she recognized the voice of the old male. A hunt was started that needed all the pack. They were certainly after the light-brown creatures with the white rumps, the antelope.

After that, Coyote did not know what was going on in the desert. She could not see the herd of antelope rushing straight to a faraway part of the plain, the wolves strung out behind on their trail with the old male loping in the lead. The wolves would not try to overtake them just yet, for a better time would come when they circled and could be cut off.

The antelope had started away at their top speed of fifty-five miles an hour, but had soon steadied this pace down to thirty-five. They could keep this up for a long time and on the plains could outrun any coyote who was not aided by others of his tribe. Cactus thorns did not hurt their hoofs nearly as much as they did the softer feet of the wolves. But if they circled, the wolves were sure to cut across to try to intercept them, and one wolf would chase hard while others loafed along and took his place, one at a time, when he tired.

The antelope continued to run with the old male following fiercely in the lead. And this time they were going straight toward their favorite range. There was no circling, no indecision. They had been chased many times in the past.

Behind the old wolf loped the pack, becoming more and more discouraged as the pace continued. They were very thirsty, so they began to tire of the chase. The old male, however, kept resolutely, grimly on. He was not one to give up easily.

Presently his mate stopped in her tracks. She had had

enough. The young wolves gathered around her, very ready to turn back to get water. They were panting hard. Their mother sniffed the trail, walked along it a few steps, howled twice, then began to retrace her steps. And all the young ones went with her. She had warned the old male and thought no more about him. It was a long trek back to the trough, but so anxious were they to have water that they loped most of the way. They did not hesitate at the water as did the antelope. They rushed to it and at once began to lap, standing side by side.

Coyote heard them and was more than ever on the alert. Then she heard something else. It was the thump of hoofs. The pack had found the two goats, who did not try to run far. They made a short circle, then stood their ground with heads facing the enemy and their backs against the door of the goatshed.

Warily the inexperienced young wolves made dashes at them, only to retreat quickly when one or the other of the goats rose on hind legs or presented her hard head. Only the white one had horns. The goats were brave enough though very frightened. Inside the shed the others, well knowing that something serious was happening, were milling around and bleating.

Coyote was running around and around her pen. Some protective instinct had been aroused in her by the plight of these ranch animals. She tried her best to climb the wire or tear it open with her teeth. She did climb it in one of the corners, only to be met by a roof of wire that threw her back. But that wire had bent and she knew at once that it was not as strong as the wire in the sides of the pen.

Meanwhile the fight had continued. There could be

only one ending. Sooner or later the wolves would close in. Coyote in her wild running did not lose sight of the wolves or of the goats. Her feeling that the ranch had to be protected was growing. She was climbing oftener now and tearing at the wire overhead. Her lips and gums were cut but she kept on working. Suddenly she saw the old female wolf come forward, shove aside the young ones, and face the goats.

The nannies saw their fate. They pressed back against the shed and waited miserably. And in front, very close now, very sure of herself, crouched the old female wolf, her ears back, her eyes never leaving the goats. Then she sprang. The brown nanny, caught helplessly by the speed of it, was gripped by her throat and thrown down. At once the white one bravely rose and came down on the wolf with her hard, sharp hoofs, but was driven off by a surge of young wolves. In excitement and joy, mad with the blood lust, the youngsters turned from her and threw themselves on the brown goat, which was down on the ground, fierce yaps coming from several throats.

That was when Coyote went mad with fury and excitement. She climbed up the side wire in three mighty heaves, stuck her nose through a mesh overhead and worked so hard, so furiously, that the mesh widened. The webbing stretched apart gradually, loosening at the joints, allowing the slender head to go through. Now it was a matter of forcing through a shoulder, and Coyote did it. The other shoulder followed, painfully. She was halfway out. Another heave and she was hanging down the side of the pen caught by her hips. Now she kicked and swung and struggled. And suddenly she was free and falling.

She landed on her head, sprang to her feet and in a few leaps was in the midst of the mass of animals. She slashed to right and left with her long teeth. On one young wolf she bore down and sent him crying into the bushes. She cut at another and met him tooth against tooth in a wild tussle that ended in his backing away with upper lip torn. The young ones were no match for her! But in front of her stood the real enemy, the jealous old female, her eyes mere slits, her teeth bared, and the hair along her back standing up straight and stiff.

How these two hated each other! Forgotten was the carcass of the goat. Forgotten, indeed, was everything except the desire to punish, to kill, to be the great queen wolf, free forever from the other's hateful presence. At that moment Coyote had indeed gone back to the wild, to the rule of fang and claw and the need to win a death struggle.

The young ones slunk to the edge of the bushes. They stayed there in a half-circle, watching, fascinated by the drama that was unfolding. Face to face in front of them stood the two older wolves, so tense that they were high on their toes, their tails nearly straight out behind them. Their lips were drawn back to show the formidable array of white fangs. They looked the same height, the same brown and gray color, the same lithe build. They seemed so evenly matched that the fight for supremacy might be a terrible one before one or the other collapsed.

Almost straight overhead the moon shone down on the scene, leaving no confusing shadows. There was no breeze, no stirring except the occasional shifting in position of the nervous young wolves. The silence of the desert night hung over all. Nearby lay the bloodstained carcass of the brown goat, and behind it, still with back against the shed, cowered the white nanny waiting for her doom.

Had the powerful old male leader appeared, things would have been different, but he was miles away still resolutely following in the dusty wake of the antelope band.

There was nothing near that could intervene to stop the conflict. The two rivals knew this, yet neither was afraid. They were wolves, with the fierce courage of their race, and they hated each other. Through the ages, this hate had led to the elimination of the weaker ones, keeping the fitter to carry on the breed.

The two moved now, slightly and very slowly. One snarled, then the other. Each was trying to gain a more favorable position. The wild one from the plains backed up a step, then another step. Coyote followed her. The wild one forgot the carcass of the brown goat and backed over it, almost tripping. That did it! The two flew at each other.

Chapter 18

A FIGHT in the wilderness can be fierce, long, and terrible. There is no referee to stop fouls, no bell to call rounds. It can go on and on without a break, usually with only the stars and the moon as an audience and they never applaud and they never hiss. The world at such times seems neutral, uninterested, waiting only to find out which combatant will survive, which will become meat for some of the many scavengers.

The two coyotes scrambled and rolled together among the creosote bushes and cacti, biting, clawing, shoving. They were too breathless to growl, too intent to see where they stumbled and fell, first one, then the other, momentarily on top. The younger wolves were scattered, scared and anxious to keep out of the fray, thinking only of saving their own necks.

Exhaustion came at last. The two lay almost side by side, occasionally snapping at each other, trying to seize a leg or any part of the adversary that was nearest. They were bleeding in places. The wild one could see only through half-shut eyes as she heaved herself forward in one final terrific effort and managed suddenly to fasten her teeth in Coyote's tender, narrow abdomen below the bulging ribs.

Coyote struggled vainly, for the other held with a grip of sheer desperation. Then slowly, painfully Coyote twisted herself until she could grasp the jowl, then the upper neck of the other. Her tiring jaws could force no dent in the tough skin and powerful muscles. She shifted lower, caught the throat and clung, chewing her way to a better, deeper hold, trying to shake and worry and choke, so that the other must release her.

The wild one's breath was cut off; it was coming in gasps—long ones. At last she had to let go of her formidable hold. Then she struggled for another one. She dragged Coyote around in a half-circle, fastened her teeth in a front leg. That way they stayed minute after minute, preparing for the next move.

The young wolves began to howl, dolefully. They were answered from the desert. The big old male was running back! He was coming fast, as if he knew that something was wrong. He came upon a strange scene in the moon's light. The young wolves were nervously trotting backward and forward far in the bushes, tails down. He passed with scarcely a glance for each. His keen nose, then his eyes, caught the tragedy in front of the goatshed. The wild female had pulled herself and Coyote to the edge of the bushes. There Coyote had finally left her, surprised that she lay without moving.

Coyote had dragged herself toward the shed, but had succeeded in gaining only half of the distance when her strength gave out. She raised her head but could move no farther, for her injured limbs and body were stiffening. The old male walked slowly from one to the other,

sniffing, studying the situation. Perhaps he had experienced things like this before; he himself had been in many
fights and had seen many others. He shook himself and
stood for a moment between the two. All his bravado was
gone. Then he walked to Coyote, sniffed her tousled
mane, pawed the earth beside her, looked in all directions,
then crouched down beside her to lick her poor bloodstained nose. She tried to wag her tail but could not.

A night can seem very long. Slowly, coldly, the moon
moved in its orbit, changing nothing except the shadows.
Coyote dropped her head. She lay there without motion.
The young wolves started back to the mountains and
deserted the place, but Coyote and the old male were

close together, he occasionally licking her wounds. Who could tell what thoughts were passing through his mind, what regrets were there, what hopes remained. Coyote looked so bedraggled and he so magnificently alive.

In the ranch house, Uncle Harry had slept badly. He had heard the bleating of the goats and the howls of the young wolves. As day broke, he dressed hurriedly and went out to see what had happened during the night. He did not know what to expect, but he was worried. The first thing he saw was the white goat backed against the outside of the shed. Then he saw the fine big form of the old male wolf rise from the ground and go slowly, reluctantly, into the bushes. He saw Coyote, and near her the body of the brown goat.

Uncle Harry stood for some time just looking and wondering. Then with quick eye he began to study the tracks in the dust. The whole story was written there. He glanced up at the hole in the top of Coyote's pen. How she must have labored to get out, he thought, how tremendous must have been her battle in defense of the goats and his property. She lay now beyond hope of his thanks. He called to his wife. When she came to the window, he asked her to hurry out and see what he had found.

Together they looked at Coyote. Unashamed, his wife fairly groaned in distress. They walked around, examining everything at the scene of the fight, the broken bushes, the many tracks, fur and blood in places.

"A whole wolf pack," Uncle Harry said with awe.

Then he glimpsed the body of the wild female, lying stretched out where she had fallen. He shook his head almost in disbelief.

"How did Coyote do it?" he whispered. "How could she defend and save one goat and dispose of an antagonist like this one—another female who must have fought like a fiend!"

One thing especially puzzled Uncle Harry: What part had the big male wolf taken? He studied the tracks once more with infinite patience and care. He found how the big wolf had walked from one to the other of the prostrate forms, then cast himself down beside Coyote. He had remained as if on guard until, as a creature of the wild, he was forced to move away to safety. Again the man shook his head in wonderment.

His wife was bending over Coyote, trying to smooth some of her coat. She straightened up suddenly and called to him.

"Coyote's still breathing!"

Uncle Harry was beside her in a moment. He took one careful look, felt the wolf's side, then started to the house on the run. His call woke the nearest veterinarian from his morning dreams.

"Come over here as quickly as you can make it!" Uncle Harry cried. "No, don't stop for breakfast or anything. Bring your kit! It's our pet wolf. She's dying. Yes, from a fight. Hurry!" Then he returned to Coyote.

"We mustn't try to move her," he told his wife. The two were kneeling beside the wolf when the doctor came hurrying from the driveway.

The doctor made a long, careful study. He felt the body, the legs; he noted the white gums, he listened to the scarcely beating heart.

"How did this happen?" he asked. "She's chewed all over. A front leg is broken. I'm sure she's bleeding internally from a terrible bite in the stomach. She can't live long. She has no blood left."

Eliza was standing back of him wringing her hands. She came forward resolutely.

"Will my blood help?" she asked quietly. The doctor looked up.

"I never heard of anything like that," he exclaimed. "I never tried such a transfusion."

"Then try it now," said Eliza emphatically. She held out her bared arm. For a moment the doctor looked puzzled. He glanced up at her and saw that she meant it.

"No one would believe this," he muttered. "A wolf! It's fantastic!"

"It's our pet who is dying for us. Hurry up!"

The doctor looked from Eliza to Uncle Harry. He ran his sleeve along his perspiring brow.

"Fantastic!" he said again.

With stethoscope against Coyote's side, he listened to her feeble heart. Beads of sweat were again showing on his forehead.

"Someone bring a blanket!" he commanded. "And warm water and some salt."

Uncle Harry brought the blanket, Eliza the water and salt. Carefully they slid the doubled blanket under Coyote and carried her to a lounge in the house.

"I'm going to try a saline solution in one of her veins," said the doctor, rolling up his sleeves. "That will partly take the place of blood.

"If this works it will make history!" he added.

"It must work!" said the indomitable Eliza.

The doctor, working carefully but expertly, applied tubing to the vein in Coyote's side and allowed the solution to enter drop by drop. It took a long time, so long that both Uncle Harry and Eliza were losing hope. Coyote had not stirred.

"She's still alive," the doctor muttered. "Why I can't see! No animal could lose so much blood and survive."

Eliza brought a moistened cloth and tried to clean away the caked dirt from Coyote's open mouth. She took such a long time that both men glanced at her questioningly.

Eliza actually was smiling.

"She's going to live!" she breathed.

"How do you know?" asked the doctor.

"She licked my hand!" answered Eliza quietly.

Chapter 19

I took a long time. The doctor worked all day, never leaving Coyote's side. He made another visit during the night. He wiped his brow many times and he muttered, "Fantastic!" many more times. When he was not busy with Coyote, he sat at a desk writing up the case in full detail. He was hoping that he would be famous. But he would never be as famous as Coyote or as deserving and devoted as Eliza and Uncle Harry.

Coyote lived. Her room was turned into a hospital. She lay on a mattress on the floor, unable to move because of her weakness, the internal injuries, and her broken leg. She ran a high fever for days and was ever restless unless Eliza sat on a pillow close by, letting her lick an extended hand. Friends of Uncle Harry tiptoed in occasionally to look and wonder, for the strange news had spread. Once again her story was in the newspapers. Photographers wanted her picture but were told to wait.

"Photograph the white goat she saved," suggested Eliza with a smile, for she was happy now.

The day came when Coyote could limp about on three legs. The injured one had been tightly bandaged with splints but would never be quite right again. The doctor came every day to check on Coyote.

"Aren't you ever going to say 'fantastic' again?" asked Eliza.

"I'm never going to stop saying it!" he answered.

Finally Coyote was allowed to limp to the out-of-doors. She stood looking out over the desert for a long time, at the creosote bushes, at the saguaro cacti standing so tall and stolidly against the line of distant mountains. She howled just once and listened, but there was no response.

Uncle Harry stood beside her wondering what she might be thinking, what dreams, what memories, were behind her soulful eyes. She was beautiful now, her coat sleek and almost shining, the light gray and the brown blending to form bright colors.

The goats showed little fear of her. They came near and bleated and the white nanny could be handed bread almost beside her.

As Coyote grew stronger, she spent most of her time walking about the ranch with Uncle Harry. Her bad leg was usable again, but she would always limp. She serenaded the coming of night with yaps and howls, the strange song of the coyote. Then she would come into the house to frisk around her benefactors and lick the hands of Eliza.

"I think she's very contented," said Eliza.

"I'm not sure," replied her husband. "Sometimes I have the feeling that she's mighty lonely."

One night, after her usual serenade, she suddenly started into the desert. This was altogether new. Uncle Harry called her but finally gave up and retired. In the morning he looked out of the window and saw her waiting in front of the house, but she was not alone. Quickly he put on his spectacles and looked again. There was no doubt about it—beside her stood a large, handsome coyote, the same one he had seen on the morning of the big fight. At the opening of the door, the wild coyote vanished in the bushes, but that night at dusk he answered Coyote's serenade.

Both Uncle Harry and Eliza watched her. She looked at them, danced around them, then vanished in the desert.

"I'm afraid we are going to lose her," Uncle Harry said rather sadly. "She seems to be turning back to the wild."

"But," answered Eliza, "she considers this her home and us her friends. She'll surely come back to us." Nevertheless Eliza, too, was doubtful.

Every day Coyote did return, usually soon after dawn. She always showed joy at being with her friends and frisked around them. She was often hungry, but occasionally she seemed to have eaten her fill.

The spring rain came and brightened the desert, and March brought endless flowers on bushes and plants and even on the cacti, and the whole brown plain seemed green and gloriously alive. There was a strange happening at the ranch. Uncle Harry found Coyote on her mattress all coiled up, a little brown coyote pup beside her, held encircled by her legs as if they were arms. He shouted to his wife and they stood regarding the scene with utmost surprise. They did not touch the little thing, though Coyote let them come very close. The pup's eyes were closed tight, but it was already covered with fur.

"What next!" exclaimed Uncle Harry. He went to the phone to tell the veterinarian, and little time elapsed before the interested doctor arrived and was viewing the mother and pup.

"Can I say it once more?" he asked.

"We'll say it for you," laughed Uncle Harry. And both he and Eliza shouted, "Fantastic!"

"After all her injuries I did not think she could do it!" exclaimed the doctor.

"Anyway, I guess that a single pup will always be the size of the litter."

"Always?" asked Eliza, laughing. "How many litters do your expect her to have?"

The doctor scratched his head. "Well," he said with a smile, "I'd say a good many. Maybe ten, judging by what I know of her age. She ought to live to be about fourteen."

"Then one each time is plenty, I think," said Eliza very firmly.

The pup throve and grew and grew. It was a male, and more and more it looked like the big old father.

"Strange things certainly are happening around here," remarked Eliza one day. "Every morning I find a dead animal on the doorstep—a prairie dog or rabbit or maybe a ground squirrel. Sometimes two of them!"

"That is the way the father coyote feeds his family," suggested her husband. "I like that."

By the middle of July the pup was a sizable wolf, and at the end of September almost fully grown, bigger than Coyote and so much like his father that sometimes in the distance they could scarcely be told apart.

Every evening the pup and Coyote sang the coyote song together and listened for the old male's answering howl. Then they would join the old one somewhere near the ranch house and go hunting. This did not make the pup shy, at least as far as Uncle Harry and his wife were concerned. He was as friendly as could be. And he was smart enough to know many unusual things, among them that the goats were not to be molested in any way. The old male learned this too, under Coyote's guidance.

These were happy days. Uncle Harry and Eliza sighed deeply when they thought about it, and wondered how long it could last. The pup meanwhile gradually took to the wild and seldom came back to the house, but Coyote never deserted them, and the big male never deserted her. One evening when Uncle Harry saw Coyote and her mate leave for the desert to hunt the rabbits, rats, mice, and gophers, he summed it up in a few words.

"If," he said to his wife, "something happens to our great pet this very night or any night, we can look back on the years and say, 'She was wonderful!' I believe that she will live long. Yes," he laughed, "and give us a new little coyote every March. Let's hope so!"

And as the years rolled by and Coyote lived to be older than fourteen, the learned veterinarian, a twinkle in his eye, summed it up in his own way with just his one favorite word—"Fantastic!"

The end.

The Author

JOSEPH WHARTON LIPPINCOTT, one of America's leading naturalists, is the author of sixteen classic stories about animals. More than fifty years of hunting, fishing, and exploring have given the author an uncanny understanding of wild creatures in their relation to mankind.

Mr. Lippincott was for many years a distinguished publisher and chairman of the board of the J. B. Lippincott Company.

The theme of this book is based largely on the author's experiences with coyotes in Wyoming, Arizona, Mexico and in Pennsylvania where a wild coyote was at large raising litters of coy-dogs for two years. The coyotes' den—a burrow—was located in the woods, a few hundred yards from Mr. Lippincott's home.